A MIDSUMMER KISS

KISS THE WALLFLOWER, BOOK 1

TAMARA
Gill

COPYRIGHT

A Midsummer Kiss
Kiss the Wallflower, Book 1
Copyright © 2019 by Tamara Gill
Cover Art by Wicked Smart Designs
Editor Grace Bradley Editing, LLC
All rights reserved.

ISBN-13: 978-0-6484133-9-4
ISBN-10: 0-6484133-9-X

DEDICATION

For those who love summer and kisses.

$\mathcal{M}$iss Louise Grant folded the last of her unmentionables and placed them into the leather traveling case that her closest friend and confidante the Duchess of Carlton—Mary to her close friends—had given to her as a parting gift. Louise slumped onto the bed, staring at the case, and fought the prickling of tears that threatened.

There was little she could do. Mary was married now and no longer in need of a companion. But it would certainly be very hard to part ways. They'd been in each other's company since Louise was eight years of age, and was sent to be a friend and companion for the young Lady Mary Dalton as she was then in Derbyshire.

The room she'd been given in the duchess's London home was now bare of trinkets and pictures she'd drawn over the years, all packed away in her trunks to be soon shipped north to a family in York. Six children awaited her there, in need of teaching and guidance and she just hoped she did well with the new position. She needed to ensure it was so since her own siblings relied on her income.

Surely it should not be so very hard to go from a lady's companion to a nursemaid and tutor. With any luck, perhaps if they were happy with her work, when Sir Daxton's eldest daughter came of age for her first Season, perchance they may employ her as a companion once more.

Certainly, she needed the stability of employment and would do everything in her power to ensure she remained with Sir Daxton's family. With two siblings to care for at her aunt's cottage in Sandbach, Cheshire, it was paramount she made a success of her new employ.

Mary bustled into the room and stopped when she spied the packed trunks. Her shoulders slumped. "Louise, you do not need to leave. Please reconsider. Married or not, you're my friend and I do not want to see you anywhere else but here."

Louise smiled, reaching out a hand to Mary. "You do not need me hanging about your skirts. You're married now, a wife, and I'm sure the duke wants you all to himself."

A blush stole over Mary's cheeks, but still she persisted, shaking her head. "You're wrong. Dale wants you to stay as much as I. Your brother and sister are well cared for by your aunt. Please do not leave us all."

Louise patted her hand, standing. As much as Louise loved her friend, Mary did not know that her aunt relied heavily on the money she made here as her companion. That without such funds their life would be a lot different than it was now. "I must leave. Sir Daxton is expecting me, so I must go." Even if the thought of leaving all that she'd known frightened her and left the pit of her stomach churning. Mary may wish her to stay, but there was nothing left for her here. Not really. Her siblings were settled, happily going to the village school and improving themselves. Sir Daxton's six children were in need of guidance and teaching and she could not let him or his wife down. They had offered to pay her handsomely, and with the few extra funds she would procure from the employment, she hoped in time to have her siblings move closer than they now were. A place that no one could rip from under them or force them to be parted again.

The memory of the bailiffs dragging her parents onto the street...her mother screaming and begging for them to give them more time. Even now she could hear her mother's wailing as they threw all their meager belongings onto the street, the townspeople simply looking on, staring and smirking at a family that had fallen low.

None of them had offered to help, and with nowhere else to go, they had moved in with her mother's sister, a widow with no children in Cheshire. The blow to the family was one that her parents could not tolerate or accept and her father took his own life, her mother only days later. Their aunt had said she had died of a broken heart, but Louise often wondered if she'd injured herself just as her papa had done.

Within days of losing her parents, Louise had been placed in a carriage and transported to Derbyshire to the Earl of Lancaster's estate. Having once worked there, her aunt still knew the housekeeper and had procured her a position through that means.

She owed a great deal to the earl's family, and her aunt. She would be forever grateful for the education, love and care they had bestowed upon her, but they had done their part in helping her. It was time she helped herself and started off in a new direction, just as Mary had done after marrying the Duke of Carlton.

"Very well." Mary's eyes glinted with unshed tears and Louise pulled her into a hug.

"We will see each other again and I will write to you every month, to tell you what is happening and how I am faring."

Mary wiped at her cheek, sniffing. "Please do. You're my

best friend. A sister to me in all ways except blood. I would hate to lose you."

Louise picked up her valise and placed it on top of one of her many trunks. "Now, should we not get ready for your first London ball this evening? As the newly minted Duchess of Carlton, you must look simply perfect."

"And you too, dearest." Mary strode to the bell pull and rang for a maid. "You're going to look like a duchess as well this evening. I have not lost hope that some gentleman will fall instantly in love with you as soon as he sees you and you will never have to think of York or Sir Daxton and his six children ever again."

Louise laughed. How she would miss her friend and her never-ending hope that someone would marry her. But the chances of such a boon occurring were practically zero. She was a lady's companion, no nobility in her blood or dowry. Perhaps she would find a gentleman's son in York, a man who would love her for the small means that she did possess —a good education and friends in high places. A man who would welcome her two siblings and their impoverished state and support them as she was trying to do.

"One can only hope," she said, humoring her. "I will certainly try, if not for my own sake, then definitely for yours, Your Grace."

Mary beamed. "That is just what I like to hear. Now, what should we do with your hair…"

CHAPTER 2

The first balls of the London Season had been taking place all week, and the Duke and Duchess of Carlton's was one of them. An event for the senses, with hot-house flowers upon every surface the ballroom could tolerate. Hundreds of candles blazed in the four chandeliers that ran the length of the room. The floor was so highly polished that one could see their own reflection in it. Nothing was spared to make Mary's debut in town as successful as the new Duchess of Carlton.

The ball was a crush, which was just what one wanted when hosting such a party. Louise stood to the side of the room, a little behind Mary, and watched as her friend and the duke stood greeting those who attended, the duke's hand never leaving the arch of her friend's back.

She smiled at their love and turned to watch the *ton* at play. As much as she had to think of her future, her brother's and sister's future and security, she would admit that she would miss this life. Being a companion did have its advantages, and she rarely did menial work that would normally be required of the position. Mary would not have it.

When she reached York she doubted she would ever have a moment's peace with six children underfoot. But, if that was the price she had to pay for keeping her own family safe, fed and clothed, then that is what she would do.

The strings of the first waltz sounded and the duke took Mary's hand, leading her onto the floor. Louise stepped forward, taking Mary's champagne. "Enjoy," she said to her friends, content to simply watch.

A tittering flittered through the bystanders and Louise turned to see the Marquess Graham, the Duke of Carlton's closest friend, bow to Lady Clara Quinton, eldest and only daughter to the Duke of Law. The young debutante waved her silk fan with a floral design before her face, her eyes coy as she pretended to make up her mind to dance with him or not.

Louise rolled her eyes. There were few who would not dance with the marquess, herself included. The man was beyond handsome, he was almost too pretty in fact for her palate. If such a thing were possible. His dark hair was unfashionably long, set atop his shoulders on the few odd occasions he wore it down. Tonight it was tied back with a little black ribbon and her fingers itched to pull the thread, watch it fall so she too could feel if it was as soft as she'd always imagined it.

Lady Clara gave in and placed her hand atop his, stepping out to join the waltz.

Louise watched as he pulled the young woman into his arms with expertise and in the scandalous way that had the *ton* tittering that he was going to ask for the woman's hand in marriage. They were certainly very comfortable with each other and Lady Clara was unquestionably a catch. An heiress with breeding that went back five hundred years, or so she'd been told numerous times by her ladyship's own companion at events such as these.

She sighed. How delightful it would be if there were men who looked like the marquess in York. It would indeed improve the outlook of her life if she could at least dream of one day marrying such a handsome man and be happy.

Due to the maddening crush, two women standing beside her shuffled closer to Louise. They both turned to glare at the offending people who were the cause of their annoyance. Their conversation drifted to Louise and for a moment she broke her own set of rules and listened. It was her last night in London after all, what harm would it do to eavesdrop for a moment or two?

She cast a furtive glance their way and recognized the widow, Lady Margaret Scarboro and her friend whose name escaped Louise at present. Her ladyship's tone was seething, low and trembling as she spoke of Lady Clara who danced with the marquess.

Her ladyship's friend bestowed on the dancing couple a cold stare and it stood to reason that she too disliked the marquess's choice of dance partner as much as her ladyship did. Louise wondered over it a moment. Lady Scarboro was a widow, and so it could be surmised that she'd harbored a tendre toward Lord Graham. Certainly if her ladyship's verbal assault was any indication, his lordship should not waste his time with such feeble and innocent women who'd likely bore him to death within a month of marriage.

Heat bloomed on Louise's cheeks at the insinuation of such speech. She flipped open her fan, idly cooling herself. Although she was unsure of the exact particulars Lady Scarboro spoke of, it was not hard to surmise what her words had meant. Louise stepped away, distancing herself lest anyone think she was part of such conversation.

She didn't need anything to stand in her way of leaving for York in the morning, and she certainly didn't need to leave London with the *ton* gossiping that she'd taken part in the blighting of one their brightest stars. Lady Clara smiled up at the marquess, an amused glint to her blue eyes. The young woman was in love with him, it was obvious to all who chanced a look in their direction. Certainly the gossip must be true. It would only be a matter of time before they were wed and she wished them well in their endeavors.

CHAPTER 3

*L*uke Ashby, Marquess Graham stumbled along the corridor of the Duke of Carlton's London home, counting the doors as he went. His eyes watered from too much whisky, and the passage swam like a pendulum in a clock. He halted, clasping the wall for support as the world threatened to turn topsy and fell him on his ass.

He took a deep breath, the thought of the delectable widow Lady Scarboro who awaited him in a room keeping him on his feet. All night she'd teased and touched him, the heat in her eyes enough to singe his skin at times. The candescent touches on his person left him with little doubt as to what she wanted. Her one good, hard stroke of his cock as they were seated at supper, hidden by the table top, even now made him throb.

Luke took a calming breath, forcing himself to feel up to the challenge of making her ladyship's introduction into his bed one that she'd remember for years to come, and possibly therefore allow him to do it again.

He smiled at the thought, walking on and thankfully, coming to the fifth door from the stairs, just as she'd instructed him. He glanced up and down the passage, hoping no one would miss him from the ball that was still in full swing downstairs.

A small twitch of conscience plagued him at the thought of bedding a woman in one of his friend's bedrooms, but the thought of her wrapped about him, taking him into her willing, hot body expelled such doubts.

Without knocking, he entered the designated room, and closing the door, stood at the threshold a moment, willing his eyes to focus in the dark space. He could faintly make out the shape on the bed, a dark presence in the room. No candle burned to light his way, nor was the fire stoked high enough to allow him to see clearly.

Damn it, he'd break his neck walking to the bed.

"Margaret," he whispered, creeping closer with caution. "Margaret," he said again, louder this time. Luke ran a hand through his hair. "Do not tell me she's fallen asleep," he mumbled. If that were the case his reputation for a libertine would be shot to hell and he'd never be able to face his friends at Whites ever again.

To have a woman fall to sleep on him was scandalous!

"Are you asleep? I thought we had other plans." He dipped his voice, shuffling out of his superfine coat and throwing it aside. Quickly he rid himself of his waistcoat and reaching behind his head, pulled his shirt from his person.

He reached out, grappling for the bed, and finally feeling the soft textures of the blankets, he climbed atop it. His lips quirked and his cock swelled at the slight form, lying in wait beneath him. He ran his hand along her leg, squeezing it a little and enjoying the long lines of her body.

Margaret rolled onto her back, a delectable little sigh escaping from her lips.

"I'm here, darling. Do wake up, we have games to play." Luke crawled over her fully, feeling his way to kiss her.

The moment his lips touched hers—the softest lips he'd ever felt in his life—his alcohol-confused mind recognized that something was wrong. Dreadfully not right.

The woman beneath him stilled, her lips puckered tight without an ounce of give in them. He frowned, pulling back. "Do not tell me you've changed your mind."

A scream rent the air, piercing in its intensity. He stilled, shocked at the deafening sound and lifted himself back, trying to make out who the woman screaming bloody murder was underneath him.

Luke scrambled backward, unable to get off her quickly enough. The door flew open, slamming against the wall with its force and he swore. The light from the hall beyond threw visibility into the room. The duke and duchess stared at him in abject horror and to Luke's dismay, disappointment clouded his friend's eyes.

"There has been a mistake." He held up his hand, halting Carlton's step toward him. "Dale," Luke said, bending to pick up his waistcoat and shirt. "I thought it was Margaret in the bed," he whispered, cringing as more onlookers started to build in the doorway.

He grimaced, looking back toward the bed, frowning as he tried to place the woman who glared at him, her fierce blue eyes brimming with fire. Luke slipped on his shirt, hastily throwing on his waistcoat and tying up the buttons.

"Would you look at that," a feminine voice purred from the doorway. "The Marquess Graham's breeches are open. Why sir, you are most indecent for those who can see you." Luke's fingers flew to his pants and he tied up his front falls, the hole in which he found himself growing wider and deeper by the minute.

Dear God, how would he get himself out of this mess?

The duchess entered the room, walking over to the woman. "Are you well, Louise? We heard you scream."

11

The woman cast him a dismissing glance. "I'm well, Mary," she said, shuffling out of bed. "I do not know what any of this is about. I was asleep and the next thing I know there is a terrible weight above me that reeked of sweat and spirits."

Luke scoffed. "I do not smell, madam." A voice cleared and Luke met the raised brow of his friend.

"I think that is not the point, Graham."

Shit. Luke glanced at the ceiling, anywhere but the many faces watching what was at play from the door. The duke walked over to everyone. "Do go back to the ball. We will join you all shortly."

Margaret, Lady Scarboro, stepped forward, blocking the duke from shutting them out. "I hope the marquess is going to do what's right and offer for the girl. To ruin someone so callously, an innocent with siblings to consider." Margaret shook her head and Luke fisted his hands at his sides. *How dare she.* It was her that he was supposed to meet, and now she was playing the honest and honorable card. That was rich coming from a woman renowned for cuckholding her husband during their marriage.

Those about her ladyship mumbled their agreement, staring at him as if waiting for him to do just that, kneel down and propose. He would not! Luke glanced at the duchess who had placed a dressing robe over the woman beside her. The girl wasn't a debutante, and although he'd seen her before he could not remember where.

The duke shut the door with a resounding bang, but he didn't avert his attention from the duchess or her companion who spoke in hushed, rapid tones.

"Lady Scarboro did not seem to know that you were meeting her. If I can trust what she'd just stated at the door about you." The duke walked over to the hearth and sat in the wingback chair. "But I would believe you over her ladyship.

12

Her history of being deceitful leads to such a surmising. Even so, you and Miss Grant have been found in bed together, with your front falls open, no less. Tongues are wagging as we speak and if we're to limit the damage to Miss Grant, there is only one solution that I can see."

"I will not marry her."

"I will not marry him."

Both their words merged into one refusal and Luke heaved a sigh of relief that he wasn't about to be hitched to a woman he did not know, or had ever heard about within the circles that he graced.

He shuddered at the idea of marrying, of having a wife and possibly children in the future. Having been orphaned at an early age, he no longer needed such support and had grown up relying on himself for most things. His grand-mother was always there, hovering like a ghoul, but she too was gone now and he was on his own.

Just as he preferred it to be.

Marriage did not fit in with his plans.

The duke stared at him, unmoved, and panic clawed across his skin. "You know I never plan to marry, Carlton. We will explain that I simply entered the wrong bedchamber and be done with this mess."

"You will not be done, though, will you, Graham? The *ton*, at this very moment, will be spreading across town what they saw here tonight. My wife's friend's reputation will be ruined."

Luke spied his coat jacket and, picking it up, shuffled into it. The young woman's face was pale, her dark-blue eyes wide with the announcement that her reputation was lost. Guilt assailed him, but he forced it aside. He should never had agreed to come upstairs to have some fun and games with Lady Scarboro.

Her ladyship's smugness flashed before his eyes and his

own narrowed. Had she planned this for him? Had she schemed to force his hand with a woman who was far removed from him in his social standing?

"You're suggesting that I marry her." Luke took a calming breath. This could not be happening.

"If you do not, Miss Grant will be ruined." The duke came over to the fire, holding his gaze. "You're better than this, Luke," he said, using his given name. "You must do the honorable thing."

He swallowed the bile that rose in his throat. The room closed in around him, his skin prickled before a cold sweat ran down his spine. He'd never wanted to marry. Such a road led to heartache and despair and he would not put himself through that emotion again.

The duchess and Miss Grant spoke quietly beside the bed, Miss Grant glaring at him with any opportunity that was afforded her. He stared down at his feet, cringing. Whatever would he tell his cousin? They had made a promise, a pact that the title would go to his relative, his heir upon Luke's death. A wife meant the possibility of children, of a family of his own.

He ran a hand through his hair. The idea repulsed him. If indeed he did find out that he was tricked into this scheme by Lady Scarboro he would ensure she was ostracized by the *ton*.

"Miss Grant, it seems that my error has led to us being placed into a position of matrimony. I will marry you and I apologize for any trouble this may have caused you. It was not my intent."

He cast a glance at Miss Grant, watching as the duchess spoke into the young woman's ear. The woman was not unfortunate in appearance, her hair was a pretty deep-russet brown color and her eyes were large and round, perfectly shaped brows arched over them. Her full lips were set into a displeased line, but even that position revealed two dimples on either side of her cheeks.

No, Miss Grant wasn't so very bad in relation to her looks, but her breeding, her non-existent dowry. Well, that was another matter entirely.

He would never live down this mistake.

She sighed. "Very well," she said, raising her chin. "I will marry you, but only because I'm being given no other choice. Do not expect anything from me."

Luke raised one brow. The word *prickly* floating through his mind. "Good, because you should not expect anything from me either."

The duke clapped his hands, drawing Luke's attention back to him. "It is done then. You are betrothed."

CHAPTER 4

a week passed and still the marquess had not returned to marry her. He'd left a missive for the duke telling him he'd gone to Doctors Commons in London to procure a special license from the Archbishop of Canterbury. A procedure that may take some time and a hefty amount of guineas if what Mary had told her was true. Even so, a week did seem overly prolonged, even to Louise.

She sat alone in the duke and duchess's drawing room. A book lay closed and unread in her lap, her ability to do anything other than think about the Marquess Graham impossible.

At this very moment she should be in York, starting her new life and ensuring the safety of herself and her siblings. She sighed, placing the book on a nearby table and standing. Her letters to her family should have reached Sandbach by now and they would know their situation had changed.

Over the past week Louise had ample time to think about her change in circumstance and a small part of her, the common sense part was happy that marriage was imminent. Her brother and sister would return to town to live with her, and she could possibly secure them a better future than she could've given them before. Give them the life that their parents had not been able to. A life where one did not need to worry about whether they would eat dinner that evening or not. If they were able to order a new winter coat or boots.

It had been better for them all from the moment her aunt had procured her the position with the Earl of Lancaster, but still, Louise had always wished for more for them. They were good people and deserved only the best.

Her mind wandered to the marquess. A marriage to such a powerful man within the *ton* had never been her goal. A simple country gentleman would've suited her very well. He was so very well-regarded in the higher echelons of Society, even if he did have a wicked reputation when it came to women. She shivered, unsure if she would be able to meet his standards both within Society and in his bed.

As a companion she was always there and yet excluded. Not part of the set or seen, rarely spoken to and mostly ignored by the society in which she circulated. Of course, Mary had never treated her in such a way, had always tried to include her and ensure she was happy, but Mary's friends had not, and it had been easier to meld into the silk wallpapers than to cause raised brows when she imparted information or an opinion on a subject that they did not see her fit to know about.

A footman in bottle-green livery knocked and entered the room. "A letter has arrived for you, Miss Grant."

She took the missive, recognizing the seal to be Sir Daxton's. Louise broke the seal and read the missive quickly.

M iss Grant,
We have received word that you were found in a compromising situation with the Marquess Graham. Please take

*this letter as termination to our agreement for you to travel and
work for my family. As a Christian man I shall take this opportunity to express that your sins will not be forgiven by God and I
suggest you repent such behavior and seek forgiveness before your
soul is doomed for eternal damnation.*

Sir Daxton

"*W*ell," she said aloud, reading the note again to
ensure she understood what she read. She had
written to Sir Daxton, explained her situation had changed,
but obviously he'd heard the scandalous part of her betrothal.
The marquess had sent out a notification in the paper that
they were to be married. Obviously not soon enough if she
was to receive such missives from people in York of all
places. Was the whole of England in possession of her
downfall?

Damn the marquess and his inability to keep from
sampling the female flesh for one evening.

Had his lordship actually ruined her then she could
understand such reactions from people, but to be accused,
shamed for an event that was none of her doing was unac-
ceptable. She was still a maid for heaven's sake.

Mary strode into the room, male voices accompanying
her. Louise turned to watch as the duke and Marquess
Graham entered close on Mary's heels. Glancing past them
all, she spied an elderly man with thin graying hair brushed
flat on his head with the help of some sort of pomade to hold
it in place. His lined face had seen many years, and he
waddled into the room with a decided limp.

"Prepare yourself, Miss Grant. We're about to be
married." The marquess came up to her, looking her over as
if she were some horseflesh he was inspecting for his stable.

"Not the finest gown, but under such circumstances, that will have to do."

"Graham," the duchess chided, taking Louise's hand and squeezing it a little. "Don't be so blunt. If you've not forgotten the whole reason my friend is in this predicament is because you could not behave yourself for one night."

Louise sniffed, lifting her chin. "I was thinking the same thing before you joined me."

The marquess took her hand, placing it on his arm, and walked her over to where the priest waited for them before the fire. Louise looked down at her hand atop his arm. Her fingers were gloveless, her having not thought she'd need them in the drawing room today. Had her mother been here she would've been so terribly aghast that she hadn't worn gloves on her wedding day.

Fear shot through her at the realization. This was her wedding. She was marrying the Marquess Graham, which meant tonight would be her wedding night. She swallowed, her heartbeat loud in her ears and drowning out the priest's words.

The priest mumbled through the ceremony, and Louise, as if hearing herself from a far-off distance, answered when required. It all happened very quickly and soon enough the priest was pronouncing them husband and wife. The marquess stared down at her and she raised her chin, ignoring the fact that she would not have been the type of woman he would've ever married under normal circumstances.

She may not be a diamond of the *ton*, a woman of wealth and good bloodlines, but she was also not to blame. They were in this position because of the rogue before her, and it was his fault that he'd had to marry a woman of no rank or anything else.

Her breath lodged in her throat and for a moment she

thought he might lean down and kiss her. Instead he turned, shaking the duke's hand and accepting a kiss on the cheek from Mary. That his smile was lackluster should not hurt, but it did. She'd told him herself not to expect anything from her, and he should not.

Still, to be so undesirable was not what a bride, no matter the circumstances, wished to feel on her wedding day.

"I think champagne is in order to toast to the new Marquess and Marchioness Graham," the duke said, turning to a footman nearby and requesting the beverages.

The footman did as he was bade and within minutes a crystal flute was handed to each of them. Mary held up her glass, smiling. "To the happy couple. May you only have bliss and," Mary pinned the marquess with her gaze, "may you know what a gift you've been given this day."

Heat rose on Louise's cheeks and she glanced down at her shoes, anywhere but the marquess or the duke whom she had no doubt was willing his wife to behave. Louise almost snorted at the idea. Mary was not one to be told what to do.

The champagne was cool, fruity and refreshing and the nicest thing that had happened to her so far this day. She furtively took in the marquess. He wore a day suit of royal blue. His cravat drew the eye to his lordship's neck, and the wide shoulders that followed. He was a tall gentleman, a man without fault some would say, but he did have a fault.

And it was her. His marriage to her.

Louise finished her drink. "Am I to stay here, Lord Graham or am I to move to your townhouse today?" There was little point in not discussing the elephant in the room. Her and her sleeping arrangements. She would of course prefer to be traveling to York instead of being married to such an ogre. This was not the type of marriage she'd thought to have for herself. Even if she'd only married a man of little means, she'd always hoped there would be affection between them. No amount of money in the world—and the marquess had quite a lot of it from all accounts—could make anyone happy.

His eyes widened and it wasn't hard to tell he'd not thought that far ahead when he'd decided today was the day they would marry.

She raised her brow. "Should I have my trunks sent over or would you prefer another night as a betrothed and not a husband?"

Mary chuckled and turned it into a discreet cough. The duke glanced at his wife, shaking his head.

"You shall return with me, of course. Mary will have your things sent over directly. I have already hired a lady's maid for you and she'll attend you upon arrival."

It was Louise's turn to be surprised, but she schooled her features, not wanting him to know she'd not thought it possible of him thinking of anyone else but himself. "Very good."

The marquess glanced between them all and Louise felt very little inclined to help him fill in the awkward silence that had fallen between them. The situation was not ideal and as no one was particularly happy about what took place not a half hour ago, one was not inclined to celebrate.

"Well then, I suppose we should be off," he said, placing his champagne glass on the table.

Louise nodded, turning to Mary and the duke. "Thank you for all you've done for me over the years, Mary. I will always be grateful."

Mary waved her thanks aside, pulling her into her arms. "None of that. We've always been sisters and we shall continue to be so even after our marriages."

Louise returned the embrace, blinking to stem the tears that threatened at having to leave her friend, her home and a place where she'd always felt welcome and respected. To leave and travel with Lord Graham, enter a home where the servants no doubt knew the dubious start to their union would be humiliating. They probably thought she'd trapped and tricked the marquess.

"Remember, Louise, to be true to yourself and the marquess will soon see that he has married a rare gem among the paste littering the *ton*."

Louise chuckled. "We shall see I suppose, but in any case, I shall make the most of the marriage and try my best."

Mary let her go and they started toward the door where the duke and marquess had already walked through. "I know you will and I hope with all my heart that you find happiness. I know this is not what you wanted, and I'm sorry this has happened, but also another side of me, a selfish side I suppose, cannot help but be thankful that I'll have you in town. A neighbor across the park in fact."

"That close?" Louise said as they made the front steps.

Mary pointed across Grosvenor Square to the row of townhouses across the green. "The marquess lives in that large property with the black door, so we shall see each other regularly and I do want to see you as often as possible."

Louise smiled. "I know, and thank you. I shall call on you later this week and we shall have tea."

⚜

*L*uke studied Miss Louise Grant, now Louise Ashby, Marchioness Graham who sat across from him in the carriage, her attention fixed somewhere outside the window. He had thought over the day, their wedding and ultimate marriage he'd be stuck with until his death and he'd come up with a plan that would suit all those involved. Even Louise he was sure.

He would take her out to his country estate in Kent, settle

her in the Graham family seat and return to town, finish up the Season, his parliamentary duties and return to Ashby House in the fall. The carriage rocked around the corner, heading for the southern road out of London and he spied the moment she questioned their direction.

"Mary said that your home was across the park. Are we not returning there, my lord?"

He tore his gaze away from her, disliking the fact she looked quite pretty in her day gown, her eyes wide and bright with query.

"We're traveling to Kent this evening, not far from Maidstone in fact. My estate is not far from London, four hours by coach. Your luggage will arrive tomorrow."

Her brow furrowed. "But Mary said… That is to say I thought I was going to be living with you. In London."

He chuckled dismissively and she flinched. He ignored the pinch of conscience that he'd hurt her feelings yet again and strove to ignore his emotions. What did Louise expect, after all? He'd told her that he would give very little in the marriage and she had too. This was no love match, or even a mild affection match. They were simply two people who had been forced to wed due to his own error of judgement and Society's narrowminded views.

He rubbed a hand over his jaw. To be forced to wed simply because he'd entered the wrong bedchamber was absurd. That he was married at all, a bona fide bachelor of the *ton*. It was well known among his friends that he never wished to marry, or beget heirs. He had his cousin set to fill those shoes and responsibilities.

His father, god rest his soul, would not be pleased by his decision in life, but he simply could not find it within himself to long for such things. Not that he wasn't fond of children—several of his friends had married and produced offspring—but to think they could be taken away within a moment of time, due to illness or an accident... He shuddered.

No. He did not want to experience such heartache.

Losing his parents and sister had been enough pain for one lifetime. He did not want to go through that again.

"She was mistaken. We're to travel to Ashby House and that is where you'll stay. Of course I shall not impose myself on you this evening, even though consummation is recommended, but we have time for such matters. You need not fear me on that score." His gaze traveled once again over her delectable, womanly curves, her delicate hands that rested in her lap without gloves. He would have to ensure that she was properly attired. He would have the best modiste sent from London to make up a new wardrobe for her. No wife of his would be shabby and without fashion sense.

Her eyes flashed fire. "I'm not afraid of you, my lord. You may sleep with me or you may not, it makes little difference to me."

He turned his full attention to her. A light, rosy hue kissed her cheeks. He bit back a smile. She may speak forward and without shame, but her words had embarrassed her a little.

"Do you wish for me to come to you tonight? I will of course, but not without your approval. It would be no chore, I can assure you, and I promise to make it worth your while."

She shifted on her seat, giving him a dismissing sniff. "I shall pass, my lord. But thank you for your kind offer in any case."

They rode along in quiet for a moment, the sound of the wheels on the dusty gravel road along with the coachman who spoke to the horses every now and then the only sound to break the silence. "Well, do let me know if you change your mind."

CHAPTER 5

The Marquess Graham's estate was too pretty for words, just like its master. Louise stood outside the mammoth front door. The windows flickering with the reflection of the afternoon sun was blinding. Not to mention the size of the home was, in her common opinion, simply ridiculous. Who needed homes as large as this? She took her newly minted husband's arm as he led her indoors and was sure upon entering the hall that the entire village of Sandbach's population could fit under its roof.

"Your home is very grand, my lord. Very beautiful." Her eyes darted everywhere, unable to comprehend that she was now mistress of such a grand estate. Gold-lined paintings of the marquess's family hung on the walls, delicate furniture sat in corners and before windows. The curtains hung the full length of those windows, billowing upon the marble floor. Opulence was everywhere she glanced about, trepidation running through her that she'd fallen into the role of wife and caretaker of all these fine things left no small amount of fear.

The staff lined up before the staircase and his lordship

introduced her to everyone in a matter of minutes. Louise tried to remember who was whom, but with so many of them it would take her many weeks before she would be able to memorize each of them.

"And this is our housekeeper, Mrs. Dunn. She'll ensure you know your way about and what is required of you as mistress of the house."

Louise clasped the older woman's hand. "It's lovely to meet you, Mrs. Dunn. I think I shall rely on you quite a lot after seeing the marquess's home."

The housekeeper's eyes widened and darted between her and the marquess. "Shall we go upstairs? I will show you to the marchioness's rooms if you like."

Luke gestured for them to go, before he turned and started for the door. "Are you not coming with us?" Louise asked, halting her steps.

He took his time in turning around to face her. "Apologies, my dear, but I have business in town. Mrs. Dunn will ensure you're settled and well cared for. I shall be back when I'm able to get away from London."

Louise kept her attention on the marquess as he turned about and left, closing the door with a decided bang and seemingly putting an end to their newly minted marriage also. She gritted her teeth. How dare he do such a thing to her? It was not her fault they were in such a predicament. If he'd only been able to keep his desires in check both of them would be living the life they both wanted.

A little voice taunted that this life was a lot better than the one she was going to have in York. To be nursemaid and tutor to six children would have been taxing for anyone. Not to mention being away from Mary and her siblings would've also been trying. At least married to a marquess gave her freedom to better care for those she loved.

"Come, my lady. I think you should see your rooms.

When we received word that the marquess was marrying, he instructed us to prepare your rooms. He ordered new curtains and linens for the bed. No expense spared and I must admit to thinking the room is quite the prettiest in all the house."

Louise pushed all thought of the marquess—Luke—from her mind and followed the housekeeper. The upstairs to the home was no less extravagant than the downstairs, and the staff bustled about, lighting and changing candles, placing hot-house flowers in vases, some swept and dusted the many pieces of furniture the marquess owned. The house was a hive of activity, a place of employment for many it would seem.

"How many staff does the marquess have at this estate, Mrs. Dunn?"

"This is the largest estate of the marquess and he has eighty-five at last count. But bear in mind that includes gardeners, stable hands, gamekeeper, those types of trades. It's not all house staff I should mention."

Louise mulled over the number. If there were eighty-five people here, how many people across all his estates did his lordship have? And now she too was responsible for these workers, and in turn, their families who relied on them. "Please be assured that if there is any issue with anything that any of the staff have, any concern at all, do not hesitate to come to me. I will always be available to them."

Mrs. Dunn stared at her a moment, before she nodded, a small upturned twist to her lips. "Thank you, my lady. I shall endeavor to do so."

They came to a stop before a set of double doors. Mrs. Dunn turned the handle and pushed them open, revealing the room. Louise gasped, stepping into the great space, at a loss for words. For there were no words to describe such a beautiful space. The marquess had not spared expense with redecorating her suite, as Mrs. Dunn had mentioned. Pastel colors covered the chairs, the bedding and curtains. It was as if summer had kissed the room and left it blooming. Flowers of the same soft color palette sat atop her mantle, and a small, round table with two small chairs sat beside the large bank of windows. A pretty place to write letters perhaps.

Louise walked over to the windows and looked out on the vast property beyond. Lawns for as far as the eye could see spread out before her, a river, flickering under the summer sun ran between the trees beyond and she sighed, a feeling of peace, contentment and happiness overflowing her. This was her home now. She was a marchioness.

Oh, the wonderful things she could do with that position.

"Mrs. Dunn. I have two siblings who live with my aunt in Sandbach, Cheshire. Please have two more rooms cleaned and prepared for their arrival. They'll be here within the week."

"You have siblings, my lady?" Mrs. Dunn beamed at the news. "Oh, it's been many years since we've had more than his lordship under this roof. To have a wife and her siblings. Well, that is wonderful, my lady."

"My brother and sister are both fifteen, almost sixteen. They've been living with my aunt for some years. I'm sure you've probably heard already that I was the Duchess of Carlton's companion prior to marrying the marquess." Louise saw little point in trying to hide who she was, she had nothing to be ashamed about in any case. "I could not have my siblings with me then, but I certainly can now. I know my aunt would like to travel and has not been able to due to her commitments with my siblings. But that can change now and if I'm to be here at Ashby House without the marquess, I shall have my siblings here instead."

"So they shall live here permanently?" Mrs. Dunn asked, her eyes bright.

"Yes, they will." And if the marquess had any issue with her inviting her family to stay, he could come out to Kent and tell her himself. Louise untied her bonnet and slipped it off, placing it on a nearby chair. "What I've seen of the house so far is simply beautiful. Will you show more of it to me before dinner?"

Mrs. Dunn bobbed a quick curtsy, gesturing toward the door. "Of course, my lady. Please follow me."

Louise stepped out of the room, no longer Miss Louise Grant, a lady's companion. Instead, she was the Marchioness Graham. And if she could not have the affection of her husband, she would at least gain the affection of his staff.

✦

*L*uke rode hard atop his mount toward London, needing to distance himself from his bride. A woman whom he had every right to lay claim to, to take into his bed and bed her good. Instead, he hauled back to London as if the devil himself were after him.

And perhaps he was. At least the female version of the archangel.

Town was not so very far away, and within a few hours the outskirts of London started to pass him by. He was thankful for it. Tonight he had the Clinton ball that he'd been looking forward to attending. Even if he were only married hours ago, that did not mean that his life should alter or stop simply because of a woman.

He cursed the mistake that led him down this path. If he happened upon Lady Scarboro this evening, he would demand she own up to her part of his downfall. For he had fallen. He shook his head. *Married.* Not only married but married to a woman with no rank or lineage. A lady's companion.

It wasn't to be borne.

But somehow he must. Luke pushed his mount on, determined to continue with his life as was, and be damned the weight that now hung about his neck. With Louise settled at Ashby House she would be well cared for and happy, as he shall be in town.

She expected nothing and he in turn wanted nothing. Of all the marriages he could have had, at least in this respect it was tolerable.

CHAPTER 6

One month later

*L*ouise sat in the drawing room and read for the second time the latest missive from Mary. Her friend was decidedly annoyed and put out at the marquess, who she reported went about town as if he'd not married at all. Mary begged her to return, to take up her place as his wife at his London home and put to rest the rumors that the marquess had continued his life of carelessness as if he were still a bachelor.

"I think the duchess is right," her sister Sophie said, staring at her with an annoyed air. "Who does this new husband of yours think he is? He cannot go about town just as he did before. His life has changed. He has a wife."

Louise sighed, folding the missive and slipping it into the small pocket on her gown. Sophie was right of course and so was Mary. The marquess from all reports was making a farce of their marriage. And as poor as she was, as low as she'd been on the social sphere, she was now a marchioness and that at least gave her a voice. A voice to stick up for herself and the future she wanted.

"You ought to march into London and show the marquess you'll not put up with such treatment," her brother Stephen said, striding into the room. He wore a newly purchased riding jacket and pants and his knee-high boots gave him an air of a country gentleman.

Within a week of being at Ashby House, Louise had her siblings brought to stay, and over the past month all of them had transformed somewhat to the people the world expected them to be. At least outwardly they suited the accommodations they now called home, even if Louise felt like an interloper every minute of every day.

Hence why she'd not traveled to town when Mary wrote to her asking where she'd disappeared to. To enter the *ton*, walk side by side with the very people she once worked for, a companion, an invisible woman behind a one of means, was not something that Louise thought she could do.

Nerves twisted in her stomach at the thought of being so bold and she stood, coming to join Sophie on the settee before the unlit hearth.

"The marriage is not one in the truest sense. I did not expect anything from the marquess and he in turn did not want anything from me."

"So what?" Sophie said, raising her brows. "Things change and what...you're expected to rusticate here in Kent for the rest of your young life, alone and without the prospect of children because the marquess cannot give up his wayward lifestyle?"

"Sophie, lower your voice, the staff will hear you," she chided.

"Let them hear us," her brother cut in. "We ought to pack you up and leave. We'll come with you, Louise. The marquess needs to know that he's no longer a bachelor. That he has a wife, my sister, and I'll not let him treat you in such a way." Her brother stared into the dark hearth, his fingers tapping idly on the marble mantle. "I thought these toffs had honor. Your husband doesn't seem to have any."

Louise let all that her siblings were telling her sink in. Over the last few days they had stated this exact plan multiple times. They were angry with the marquess, she could understand that, but to travel to town, to invite themselves into his home felt wrong somehow. "What if we travel to town and he refuses to let us stay?"

Stephen threw up his hands. "Let him try. You're his wife, not some wench off the street. And if he does treat you with so little respect, I shall call him out and put a bullet through his cold heart."

Louise stood, coming over to her brother and taking his hand. "When did you become so honorable and sweet? You're a good man. Do not ever change."

He leaned down and kissed her cheek. "I shall never change, but as for your husband, he certainly needs to before he loses the wonderful gift that is our sister."

Sophie came over and hugged her about the waist. "If you go to town, we shall come too. We shall support you in winning the respect of the *ton* and their lofty prejudices. The marquess has a wife, and so he now needs to act like a husband."

She smiled at her siblings. How she had missed them and their encouragement. If her marriage was a disaster, at least it had enabled her to have her siblings back under her roof. To be able to feed and clothe them without the worry that circumstances may change that could jeopardize that.

"I have no wardrobe for town. I know the marquess sent a modiste to us here in Kent, but she only gave me a few gowns to get about the house and estate. I have nothing suitable for a London Season. However will I afford such a thing?"

Sophie smirked, seating herself back down on the settee. "You charge everything to your husband of course, silly. He'll pay for everything. And if you don't, I certainly will make sure everything that you purchase is of the highest quality and the most expensive item in the store. We will shock him out of his bachelorhood that way if we must."

Louise wasn't so sure such an idea would be a good one. What would the marquess say when he started to receive such bills? He had not wanted her as his wife and so now to have to pay for her gowns could be a bitter pill to swallow.

"I doubt the marquess would like that," Louise said.

"Good," her brother declared, ringing the bell pull and ordering tea. "I hope he does not. After his treatment of you this past month, sending you away as if you're a dirty little secret, I hope the bills from London's best modiste, boot makers and milliners pricks his conscience that he's been a dreadful bore and ungentlemanly in his treatment of you."

Louise clasped her roiling stomach. Could she do this? Could she return to town and be the woman worthy of the title of marchioness? She was educated, well-versed in how people were to behave in polite Society. Her best friend was the Duchess of Carlton for heaven's sake.

She nodded as fire singed away the nerves in her stomach. "Very well. We'll return to town and I'll enter the Season. It's my right, after all. And if the marquess does not like it, I'll simply ask Mary if we may stay at her house until Season's end."

Sophie clapped, her long, golden locks giving her the air of an angel, although her soul was as strong and determined as a fallen one. "We'll leave as soon as we can organize ourselves, no more than two days I should think. And then, my lady, you shall show that husband of yours that to treat a Grant in such a lowly manner is not recommended."

"No, it's not," her brother piped in, thanking the footman who brought in a tray of tea. "He'll soon learn that you're not to be tossed aside as if you're worthless. It's his fault you've had to marry him. The Grants are fighters and if you want more from your marriage, even if that more is only children, then you deserve that happiness. Do not let this little hiccup at the beginning ruin your future."

Louise stared at her siblings. When had they grown up and become so knowledgeable and supportive? She nodded, determination thrumming through her veins. "You are both correct. I'll inform the staff we're to travel to town. Let us see if we can make a splash big enough to be noticed."

Sophie laughed. "Oh, you'll make a splash all right, and it'll be big enough to drown the marquess."

If only... At least, Louise would certainly try.

*T*hey arrived in town three days later and thankfully settled themselves into the Marquess Graham's London townhouse without incident. In fact, upon arrival they were told that the marquess was not in residence, was in fact staying at his flat that was closer to his gentlemen's club, Whites.

It should not have surprised Louise that he would opt for a smaller residence. Even so, her fear of being so bold as to come to London had well and truly been replaced with annoyance that her husband would treat her in such a way.

The staff at their London home seemed as pleased as those at Ashby House to have someone to attend to. After the housekeeper Mrs. Ellis had shown them the house, and introduced the staff, Louise had opted for tea in the front parlor, wanting a moment alone. She sat down at the ladies' writing desk and pulled out a piece of parchment, quickly writing a missive to Mary that she'd arrived in town. She invited her friend to attend her outing tomorrow and begged her for assistance to help her with her first foray into the *ton* as the Marchioness Graham.

She rang for a footman using the little golden bell on her desk. He entered within a moment, bowing. "You rang, my lady?"

"Please have this letter sent directly over to the Duchess of Carlton's home. Also, I need a carriage tomorrow morning. We're going shopping and I'll need its services most of the morning and possibly the afternoon."

"Of course, my lady." The young man dipped into a curtsy and left, the soft click of the door loud in the sizeable room. Louise took a calming breath. She could do this. She was not an interloper or unwelcome here. She was the Marchioness Graham and no matter what her husband thought of that detail, she would show him that she was here to stay and that no one made a fool of her.

Especially when none of this was her fault.

👑

*T*heir shopping expedition was unlike any Louise had ever experienced in her life. The shop assistants went above and beyond to help her and the duchess in choosing the full wardrobe of evening gowns, day gowns, morning and riding ensembles. Colors that suited her dark hair and fair skin. Nothing that left her washed out or looking sickly. When holding up the deep reds and greens, she had almost looked like a different woman. Gone was the lady's companion, and in her place stood a marchioness. A woman who in her own right had power within the *ton*, whether the Society she now graced liked it or not. She was here to stay and she would not let anyone, not even her husband, look down on her and her common beginnings.

Had she not had such a humble start in life, she would not be the generous, caring woman she was. Which, in her estimation, was a lot better than those born to wealth that cared nothing for the common man or his struggles.

After her gowns, hats, caps and bonnets were ordered from the modiste and promised within a fortnight, they had gone on to purchase a riding hat from a gentlemen's hat maker. They visited shoemakers and ordered slippers and evening shoes. Reticules, gloves, muffs and shawls were ordered, all to suit the different gowns and outings she'd attend.

To celebrate their afternoon of shopping, of fun and plenty of laughter, they had traveled to Gunthers and tasted sweetmeats, pastries and fruit ices. The outing together had given Louise a chance to catch up with the duchess, whom she'd not seen since her marriage to the marquess. And allowed the duchess to get to know Louise's sister Sophie who accompanied them.

"You're going to look beautiful at the Kirby ball next week," Mary declared, smiling. "Madame Devy has assured you the sapphire embroidered gown will be delivered by then. As much as I care for Lord Graham, his treatment of you is intolerable and I'm looking forward to seeing him eat humble pie."

Louise took a sip of her tea, enjoying its rejuvenating qualities. "I'm sure I'll see him before the ball. The accounts he's to receive in the coming days will no doubt alert him to my arrival in town. The size of the bills may ensure I see him sooner rather than later."

Mary and Sophie chuckled. "You may be underestimating how much you're worth now, my dear. The Marquess

Graham's estate is one of the richest in the country. I believe Cavendish is on equal bearing with your husband's wealth." Her friend threw her a mischievous grin. "The accounts may alert him to you being in town, if your staff has not notified him of this fact already, but I do not think this is what will bring him to your door. He'll be more interested in why you've returned to London when he'd decidedly relocated you to Kent."

Louise bit her lip, the thought of facing her husband for the first time in a month making her skin prickle. He would not be pleased she'd ignored his decree and returned to London. He'd likely demand she return to Ashby House and forget about the Season altogether.

"Well, I won't be going back to the country. Not until after the Season ends at least," she said, determination cloaking her words. "I may be his wife, but I'll not be sent back to Kent like an embarrassing little secret. I cannot help but be disappointed that he's not put a stop to the talk about town about our marriage. I know he never wished to marry me, but now that he has, all due to his own tomfooleries, he should squash any talk about us. My arrival in town at least should put to rest that he'd sent me off to the country never to be seen again. Now I have to try and gain some respect within the *ton*. Not that I care what they think, but I'll not be laughed at. Not by any of them."

"I shall be right beside you too, and the duke also. The marquess and the *ton* will not stand a chance of bringing you down." Mary plopped a pastry into her mouth with a determined nod.

Louise liked the sound of that and hoped it would be so. This was her life now, no matter if she'd imagined different. She was married and the sphere in which she now circulated was exalted. That did not mean that she would lose who she was, for nothing could change her principles, but she would not let those who sought to tarnish her name to continue. The Marchioness Graham was in London, and she would not be looked down upon by anyone. Not even her husband. The marquess and the *ton* would not stand a chance in bringing her down.

CHAPTER 7

*L*uke had heard the rumors over the last week. His wife was back in London. The stiff-rumped chit had gone against his orders and returned to town. Not that he'd expressively demanded her to stay in the country, but he'd not thought she would leave their country estate for the viperish world of the *ton*.

Which, in fact, had turned out to be exactly what she'd done. And if the accounts he'd received over the past week were any indication, she was spending his money like water on a wardrobe fit for the Season.

He sat in his carriage and took a decidedly calming breath. The Kirby ball was one event they would both attend. The Duke and Duchess of Carlton had demanded his presence in support of their mutual friend Viscount Kirby who had just inherited his title. Of course he would've attended in any case, whether his wife was present or not, for he would never leave Christopher alone to face the horde of young ladies who would no doubt be looking to capture his attention. The lad was only one and twenty, too young for marriage and he would not have him become prey to the matrons of the *ton*. No matter how well they thought the young lord would suit their charges.

That his wife would also be present was merely a complication or annoyance depending on his mood. Over the last few weeks he'd pushed aside the hurt he'd registered on her face when she'd realized he was leaving her in Kent. It was his fault, after all, that they were married, she didn't deserve to be treated with his wrath. He was more angry with himself than with her. He'd placed them into this position. His selfish need for pleasure had outweighed his common sense that night and now they would both pay for his sins.

The mistake had caused ripples throughout the *ton* and of course with his cousin, whom Luke had promised the title would revert to upon his death. His relative had taken the news of his marriage reasonably well, even so, Luke had assured him that the union would not bear children and so the title would be his cousin's one day.

Luke tapped on the roof and the carriage door opened. He strode into Lord Kirby's Mayfair residence and shook his hand at the doors to the ballroom. His young friend seemed uncommonly nervous, and he supposed stepping into the new shoes of viscount and being so very young was want for some anxiety. A few whiskys would put him right.

He strode into the ballroom, the crush of people almost as oppressing as the smell of perfume and sweat. His nose twitched and he started toward the windows where at least some fresh air may venture indoors and save his senses.

Luke spotted Carlton, who seemed to have his very idea of being near a window and he made his way over to him. "Evening. Looks like Kirby had a good turnout this evening."

Carlton, thankfully on his own, his duchess nowhere to be seen, nodded. "A successful ball for his first." The duke took in his appearance before turning back to watch the dancers. "Good to see you here. I had wondered if you would stay away."

Luke took a crystal flute of champagne from a passing footman, taking a much-needed sip. "I suppose you're implying that because my wife is to attend that I would not." He glanced at his friend. "I promised Kirby I would be here tonight and I am. My wife had no bearing on the matter."

Well, a very little bearing. He was interested to see how she had fared all this time without him. How she took to the sphere in which she now circulated. Luke schooled his features as he studied those about him. He did not see Louise among the faces.

"She's not here yet. Mary is bringing her tonight, but they had a small dinner party to attend to first at Lady Scott's. A woman both the duchess and marchioness have known for some time."

Luke ignored the fact that Carlton assumed he'd been searching for Louise, he didn't want anyone to see that he was curious to see her again. Instead, he mulled over Lady Scott and tried to put a face to the familiar name. "Was she not married to a Scottish viscount? He passed away, did he not?"

Carlton smirked. "Died under his mistress for all accounts, although the family will never state such a thing publicly. You may wish to watch what Lady Scott says to the marchioness. She's not a supporter of infidelity."

People would assume, based on Luke's past behavior, that he *was* a supporter of infidelity. They couldn't be more wrong. When one was married, one ought to take their vows seriously. It was a conversation that he needed to have with his wife. He didn't want children, and she certainly did not wish for him to be her husband, so some sort of agreement would need to take place between them. He could not go the rest of his life without sleeping with a woman, so his wife would ultimately have to be his bedpartner, slake his needs, but they would have to be careful. Louise had said for him not to expect anything from her, and such a proposition suited him to a point.

Luke finished his champagne, placing the glass on the window ledge behind him.

"Have you seen the marchioness since her return to town?" Carlton asked, his attention fixed on something near the ballroom doors.

"I have not," he answered, unable to remove the indifferent tone from his voice. "I do know she's been spending a small fortune at the dressmaker's, but otherwise, no, I have not called on her."

Carlton's smirk deepened and Luke frowned. "What is it? Is there something I should know?"

The duke nodded toward the door and Luke glanced through the crowd and the breath in his lungs seized. He felt his mouth pop open and he closed it just as quickly, not willing to let anyone know that the sight of his wife left him...stunned.

The duke cleared his throat. "Who knew Miss Grant was so very beautiful."

Luke frowned, the compliment on his wife not as welcome as he thought it might be. To hear another man say such a complimentary thing didn't sit well and he adjusted his stance, schooling his features.

How was it that the young woman he'd interrupted from sleep was this dark-haired beauty, with striking blue eyes and tempting mouth. Companion or not, how had he not seen her before...

Because you were not looking close enough.

Luke pushed the thought aside, smiling a little in welcome as the duke of Carlton and his wife came to stand before them. The duchess went straight to the duke, wrapping her arm in his. Louise came and stood at Luke's side. Even from here he could feel her pulsating with anger, with annoyance at his presence. He took her hand and placed it on his arm, turning toward her.

"You look beautiful, my lady." Legally that was exactly what she was. His lady, and yet, from the hard set of her lips, her stance against him, her not being a willing participant to this farce of a marriage was obvious.

Out of his peripheral vision he took in her sapphire gown with the billowing silk skirt that did little to hide her bountiful figure or slim waist. She was nothing like he remembered, not that it changed their circumstances or his thoughts on their marriage, but at least she now looked the part of marchioness. That was something, he supposed.

A footman bowed before her, and she took a glass of wine. "How very fortunate to run into you here, my lord. How have you been, *husband*?"

Her use of the term husband startled him and he tore his gaze back to her, not missing the amused grin on her lips. "I think I'm as well as you are, *wife*." His reply merely garnered him a chuckle that ran over his skin and felt like feathers, enticing and soft.

Lord Stopford bowed before the marchioness, barely giving Luke a second look. "Would you care to dance, Lady Graham? I see that your husband has not done the right thing by you and asked, and so I thought to remedy the dissatisfaction."

She let go of his arm and stepped out with his lordship. "I would love to, thank you."

Luke smiled at their parting, and yet anger thrummed along his spine. Their marriage was not wanted by either of them, and yet the idea that she may take a lover, cuckhold him, made his stomach roil.

It should not. Only a moment ago he himself recognized

the need for them to speak about what would occur in their marriage. But the marchioness could not have a child that was not his, should the worst happen and she fell pregnant. He would never allow another man's son to inherit his title, so where did that leave them?

He watched as Louise laughed and danced with the exceedingly handsome earl. Grudgingly he had to admit that she looked beautiful in the man's arms, more so than he'd ever known. As a lady's companion he'd always known her to be about the duchess, a friend in need if required, but he'd never glanced beyond Mary's shoulder to look at who stood in the shadows.

A failing on his behalf, but he was a marquess. A man of his stature and rank within the *ton* was expected to make a marriage worthy of the title. In his case Society at large did not know he intended never to tick that box.

But now that he had, and seeing his wife dancing in the arms of another man, well, now he didn't know what the hell he was feeling at all.

"Troubled?" the duke asked, leaning close to ensure privacy. "He is but one of many who've noted your absence from the marchioness's life and seem set on remedying the situation."

He clenched his jaw, his teeth aching. "The marchioness has been making a spectacle of herself?" Not a fair question, even he would admit, but it would force Carlton to tell him the truth of the situation without looking as desperate for information as he was.

"The marchioness has been beyond reproach, and we have escorted her everywhere, and returned her home at the end of the night," the duchess inserted, her cool gaze dismissing him before she looked back toward the dance floor.

"Louise is not whom you should be worrying about.

There is a rumor about London, as you're probably already aware, that you do not intend to have a true marriage. That you were overheard at Whites as stating the union was in name only." Carlton narrowed his eyes on him and Luke felt as small as a bee. "The gentlemen who have no interest in a bride have taken that, along with your continual attachment to your bachelor residence in Mayfair, as confirmation that you do not care one whit what the marchioness does or with whom."

The duke's words rang with dread and Luke stared about the room, noticing for the first time this night that the guests glanced his way, small, secretive smiles on their lips and laughter in their eyes. Was this what people were thinking?

He sighed, adjusting his cravat. He ought not kid himself. It was his fault they were gossiping about him, his marriage and what kind of life he was willing to have with his wife.

No life at all.

Luke mulled over the complexity of the situation. The thought of having a child with Louise, while not wholly awful, left dread to churn in his stomach.

Damn the *ton* and its stipulations, its rules and censure.

"I suppose that means that I'll have to change that opinion and soon."

The duchess raised her brow, giving her husband a secretive smile that Luke did not appreciate.

"I suppose it does, and if I were you, I would do it sooner rather than later. Tomorrow would suffice."

Luke followed the marchioness's progress as she stepped off the dance floor, walking with Lord Stopford until they came to another group of gentlemen and some ladies. They welcomed her into their circle and spoke amicably.

His hands fisted at his sides as his lordship's hand sat upon her back, too familiar and too damn close. Lord Stopford laughed at something someone in the set said, and glanced Luke's way. If he registered that Luke didn't appreciate his hands upon his wife he did not show it, he merely kept his hands upon her person.

What the blasted hell was Louise thinking to allow him such liberties? She was a lady's companion, she knew the rules of what was correct and incorrect. And yet, from what he knew of the duke and duchess's courtship, maybe the woman knew when to be lax in her rules and what was appropriate for a lady in such a situation. Louise had certainly granted her charge—now the Duchess of Carlton— liberties she should not have been allowed.

Before he knew what he was doing his feet took him across the room. He charged across the dance floor, ignoring the startled *yips* and *excuse mes* as he went directly across to where Louise stood with her group of tactile *friends*.

Where were these people when she was nothing but a lady's companion? Certainly, nowhere he'd ever seen them. They had not wanted or bothered to know who the duchess's companion was and Louise should not be such a fool to be taken in by their pretty words and false friendships.

Lord Stopford raised his brow as he came up to them, and his refusal to let go of his wife sent hot anger coursing through his blood. He came about the back of Louise, taking his lordship's hand and twisting it away as he came to stand beside his wife.

Lord Stopford stepped back, his eyes narrowing, but without a word.

Good. Hopefully the bastard understood that he would not, nor would he ever allow Louise to take a lover.

"If you'll excuse us. My wife promised me this next dance," he said, smiling at the ladies. They tittered and gushed at him, as they always did, but their fawning was lost on him. His chest felt tight, and a small sweat broke out on his skin.

Luke took a calming breath, unsure why he was reacting in such a way. He'd almost committed violence against a man for actions that he himself had partaken in only a month past.

The thought shamed him. Now, with the shoe on the other foot, to see someone else take a pointed interest in what was essentially his did not sit well and he silently begged for all the husbands whom he'd given sleepless nights to forgive him.

Louise walked beside him as if nothing was amiss, and he wanted to break that icy shell she'd erected about herself. When he pulled her into his arms, there was no wilting wallflower, no hurt registering in her eyes. No anger or fear. Nothing.

He didn't want nothing. He wanted to know what the hell sort of game she was playing.

"Enjoying yourself with Lord Stopford's paws all over you? Or maybe I should ask how long you've been shagging him. You've been in London a month now, plenty of time to have a gentleman of the *ton* warm your bed."

She smiled up at him and he cursed. When the hell had she become so alluring? Had he been blind all the times he'd stood with the duke and duchess? He supposed he had been. His fixation had been on Lady Scarboro and the pretty little debutante Lady Clara, whom he liked to play and tease. Not that he would have ever married her, but it was amusing and a pleasant way to pass the time.

This woman in his arms, his wife, was punishment for all his wrongdoings. God was punishing him for being a cad.

You are a cad and you deserve everything you get.

He dismissed the voice, pinning her with his gaze. "Answer me."

"I have to have someone to warm my bed. My husband has made it abundantly clear that he will not."

He shut his mouth with a snap, pulling her close as they turned within the waltz. The music was loud in his ears and his nape pricked with awareness that all eyes were upon them. Watching and wondering what they were discussing.

If only they knew…

"You better tease, madam." His voice vibrated with temper that he did not recognize within himself. What did he care who his wife flirted with? He should not. He was not emotionally involved with this woman. Their union was a mistake. One of his making. To be so territorial with her was confounding and he growled.

"If you ventured to live with your wife, you would know. I cannot be expected to be alone for the rest of my life. I must carve out my own little bit of happiness if you shall not supply it for me."

He shook his head, pulling her closer. "You said that I should expect nothing from you. Are you a liar as well as an unfaithful wench?"

His words broke through the defensive wall a little and her eyes flared, anger making the deep blue of her irises like a fathomless, swirling sea. "I was angry and upset when I said that. You ruined me in front of the whole *ton* and then demanded marriage as if I should be grateful. Of course I said what I did. Anyone would."

The feel of her in his arms, all womanly curves, pulled at a part of him who longed for a woman in his bed. No matter what the *ton* may think, he'd not taken a woman into his bed since the night he'd walked into Miss Grant's room.

Lady Scarboro had of course tried, and failed. He was certain her ladyship was the sole reason he was married at all and he'd never take her into his bed again.

So what the hell was he going to do? Take Louise into his bed, which inevitably led to children. A family. No matter how careful one was, if a child was meant to be, it would happen.

Damn it all to hell. It wasn't to be borne.

"You want a true marriage. A family. With me."

She focused on something over his shoulder and he wanted her to look at him. Not some unseen thing behind his head. *Him.*

"I cannot have it with anyone else, can I? I'm married to you, so who else can I have such a future with?"

The scent of jasmine wafted from her skin and he breathed deeply, having always loved that fragrance above any other. She was too tempting, too sweet for him. He was a rogue. A selfish, obstinate lord who was used to getting his own way.

However was he going to deal with her?

Her statement clanged about in his head like a death knoll. How indeed…

CHAPTER 8

*T*he following morning Louise stood in the foyer of
the marquess's London home as trunk after trunk
was carried through and up the stairs.

Her sister came to stand beside her, her eyes full of
amusement. Louise, on the other hand, felt as though she
were having an out-of-body experience. The marquess was
moving in, that was obvious, but what was not so obvious
was whether he would give her the marriage she longed for.

They had been without a family for so long. With her
siblings having been separated from her, she wanted them to
be part of her new future. That the marquess was here was at
least one small step in making a go at their marriage. Surely
he wished for a child. An heir. From what Mary had told me,
he'd also been without his parents for many years. Could he
be as lonely as she'd been at times?

She clutched her fingers before her, her hands cold and
clammy. "I cannot wait to meet the marquess. Is he handsome?" Sophie asked, almost bouncing in her excitement.

"He's very handsome, but he's yet to arrive. Come," she
said, pulling her toward the front parlor that she'd taken to

using the most during the day. It gathered the afternoon sun and was warm, no matter the English weather.

They sat and had tea, the clock on the mantel clicking the minutes away, winding Louise up more and more with every passing second. Would the marquess be amenable or surly? Would he show his dislike of their situation by making her life here with him uncomfortable? Louise watched as her sister flicked through the latest fashion plates, while Louise's attention was wholly focused on the front door and of any new arrivals.

What seemed like hours passed by and then, finally, the muffled male voice and the clipped steps of someone heading toward them sounded outside the door.

Nerves pooled in her stomach and Louise stood, adjusting her dark-pink morning gown and ensuring all was in order. Her sister continued to read, oblivious to the turmoil that wracked her body.

The door flung open and in strode the marquess. He'd removed his gloves and hat, both clasped in one hand at his side. He took in the room, his blue eyes stopping on her sister. "Friend of yours?" he asked, his eyes narrowing with inspection of her.

"Lord Graham, may I introduce you to my sister, Miss Sophie Grant. Sophie, this is Luke Ashby, Marquess Graham."

Sophie's eyes widened and she stood, dipping into a pretty curtsy. "Very pleased to meet you at last, my lord."

His lordship placed his gloves and hat on a nearby table, coming to stand before the fire. "A sister," he said, turning his attention back to Louise. "Anything else that I should be aware of?"

Louise clasped her fingers before her, unsure how to tell him that she also had a brother who lived here. From the displeased line of his brow and unsmiling lips, the news of a sister was not welcome either. This was not the best start to their married life under one roof, but then, the start of their marriage was not good to begin with.

She straightened her back. "Yes. My brother is also living here. You ought to know that as well."

♛

*L*uke shut his mouth with a snap and wondered for a moment if he'd stepped into another world. Who were these people who lived here? Of course Louise had stated they were her siblings, but how had he never known such a thing about her, especially now that she was his wife?

"Would you please leave us for a moment, Miss Sophie?" he asked, smiling to buffer the annoyance he felt running through his veins. His wife, uncommonly pretty today in her dark-pink muslin morning gown, sat on a nearby settee and waited for him to speak.

No longer the wilting wallflower, it would seem.

"How did I not know that you had siblings? Or that they were living here?" Under his roof for who knows how long. He schooled his features. He was married now, the life of bachelor that he'd enjoyed so very much was over. Still, it rankled that it was the case or that he now seemed to have an instant family.

One that he'd never wanted.

"They've been living with my aunt due to our limited means. Upon our marriage, I had them travel to Ashby House to be with me. When the duchess asked me to return to town, I had them come along."

Did you now... "How old are your siblings?" he asked, curious despite himself.

"Almost sixteen, my lord. Sophie and Stephen are twins, you see."

He turned to face the fire, wanting to remove her from his vision. After their dance last evening, he'd dreamed of her. The dream had not been one that allowed sleep-inducing refreshment. Instead, he'd dreamed of stripping her sapphire gown from her body, unveiling the hidden gems beneath all that silk and taking his fill.

The morning gown she wore today seemed uncommonly fetching and not what he needed to see if he was to keep his hands off her. Ensure that they both understood what type of marriage they had and what was expected of them and what wasn't.

The image of Lord Stopford dancing with her the night before, his hands low on her back, his words close to her ear flittered through his mind and he fisted his hand on the marble mantel.

"I suppose since they are your family I'm unable to deny the request of them staying here with us. Even so, it would have been nice to have been asked."

Her eyes flared and she stood, coming over to him. "I would've asked, of course, but I did not think to see you again until the end of the Season and well, I knew my aunt wanted to travel, so I requested them to come to me. I did not mean to overstep my mark."

Luke drank her in, tall and proud before him. Her eyes were bright and clear, and uncommonly lovely. If he were to choose a woman for himself to marry he supposed someone as fetching as Miss Grant would have suited him very well. Her figure was perfectly proportioned and curvy, her gowns accentuated all the correct places one's gown ought. Her nose was small and straight and her lips...

His attention snapped to that part of her person and he stilled when her sweet, pink tongue flicked out to moisten them. Luke blinked, bringing back his thoughts from the dangerous territory where they'd wandered. He straightened his spine.

"What is done is done and if they're your siblings, I will not deny them your company." Not that he needed to be responsible for any more people, but he supposed, as the siblings were almost sixteen, they would not be long under his roof before they too sought their own paths in life. He could accommodate that. It was not so very much to ask.

"Now," he said, waiting for her to meet his gaze. "Regarding our marriage and what I expect from you."

She nodded without words and he ignored the hope he read in her blue orbs. Did she expect a true marriage? Surely not. Not after how their nuptials came to be in the first place. "We will keep to our rooms and not share a bed, for now at least." At least until he could procure a French letter to use while making a beast with two backs. "I also expect absolute fidelity from you. I will not condone you sharing a bed with any other gentleman of the *ton*. Especially Lord Stopford whom you seem to favor so very much."

His wife scoffed and he flinched. "You find such a request preposterous, my lady?"

Her lips thinned into a tight line and she watched him like a genius watched a fool. He wasn't anyone's fool. "And while I'm remaining the vestal virgin, how are you conducting yourself about town, my lord? Are you taking an oath of chastity or am I expected to turn the other way and ignore your indiscretions?"

Luke had never had a woman speak to him in such a forward manner, and bugger him if it wasn't a little amusing to see that his wife had some spark to her blood. A small backbone after all. "As a marquess and gentleman what I do is none of your concern, madam."

He stepped past her and he stilled when she gripped his

upper arm, stalling him. A shock ran through his arm, echoing throughout his body and he stilled.

What the hell was that?

"I'll not be made a fool of twice, Lord Graham. You've already bundled me into this marriage through a situation not of my making. I'll not then stand by and watch as you sleep your way through the women whom I have to entertain." She let go of his arm, attempting to throw him a little as she did so.

He didn't move an inch. "I will be discreet." The lie almost choked him and he swallowed. He would not be told what to do by a woman, certainly not a woman he did not want. Who did this chit think she was?

She raised her chin, a perfect rosy hue spreading across her dimpled cheeks. Sweet mercy, she was pretty. Prettier than he'd ever realized. His body, typically male, had a typical male response. Louise's attention drifted over him as if she sensed his train of thought and she stepped back. "No."

He followed her. "No?" he said, menace in his tone. "You do not have a choice." And she did not, as unfair as that was. An image of his parents flittered through his mind, happy and loving, his little sister playing at their feet before a roaring fire as they sat together, arms entwined, enjoying a night in watching their children play.

So long ago now since they'd left him.

"Of course I do. I will not allow you to go on with your life as you once did, my lord. I'm here, a marchioness because of you, and if I want affection in my life and my husband is unwilling to secure that for me, I will seek it elsewhere."

He clasped her upper arms, wanting to shake some sense into her. Instead, his mind diverted to how very small she was, how with very little effort he could break her. Not that he ever would, but being so near to her he once again was reminded that she was his now. If he so chose, he could seek his husbandly rights this evening and have her.

Dear God, that was tempting.

She glared up at him, all fire and ire, her eyes blazing with anger. Good, he wanted her angry at him. Anger meant she would not push him, seek him out and demand things he was not willing to give her. Such a road led to disaster and broken hearts.

He knew that better than anyone.

"No you will not."

Her breasts rose with each of her labored breaths and he fought not to glance at her bodice. "You must sleep with me. The marriage must be consummated, otherwise I see very little point in continuing this charade. An annulment would be better than this."

His fingers slid about her arms, slipping down to her elbows. His body hardened at the idea of bedding her. If she was as passionate in bed as she was when arguing with him, bedding her was not a good idea. He could get used to heat between his sheets. But she did make a good point. He had to consummate the marriage if he were to keep her.

He thought over her demand, knowing he had little option. She was his wife. He must at least sleep with her once. Nothing would come of it, he would make sure of that.

"Very well. I'll come to your room this evening."

Her mouth popped open on a small gasp and he tore himself away, striding from the room before he took her blasted delicious mouth and lay claim to her. There would be minimal kissing, no affectionate pets or words. He would keep her at a distance. Distance meant safety. She would not wheedle her way into his heart. She may have everything else that she desired—her siblings, clothing, food and jewels—but not him.

Never him.

57

CHAPTER 9

*L*ouise bathed and dressed in one of the new silk shifts that Mary had helped her pick out the other day while shopping. She sat at her dressing table, dabbing a small amount of jasmine scent on the underside of her jaw.

She caught herself in the mirror, her eyes uncommonly large and startled almost. The thought that tonight she would sleep with Lord Graham was almost too unbelievable to believe. He was London's most coveted rake. An unpardonable flirt. And he was her husband.

However was she going to be enough for him?

The idea that after tonight there would be no more nights was not acceptable. After her parents had passed away, leaving her to care for her siblings, she'd wanted to give them the family they craved. Now she could do that. Help them find their future paths, whatever that may be, become a mother herself and love unconditionally.

She'd silently hoped that her move to York may prove to be the stepping stone to such a life. To be the mistress of her own home, beholden to no one. In a way she was that now, although where she'd hoped for love, and respect in her marriage, she'd received a hasty wedding to a man who could not be in the same room with her longer than ten minutes.

Louise rose from her chair and went over to her bed, staring at the linen that had been pulled down for her in preparation for sleep. She climbed in, settling the blanket about her waist and stared at the door that led to the marquess's room. Not one sound came from the chamber and she chewed her lip, wondering if he was preparing himself. Was as nervous as she was.

Never in her life had she ever been so intimate with a man, and although Mary did tell her of some of the things that happened between a husband and wife, a lot of the time her friend had simply looked dreamy and declared that Louise would enjoy it. She would see.

At a time like this, doubts plagued her. To enjoy such a thing seemed an odd thing to do, and yet, Mary had insisted all would be well.

The door opened and the breath in her lungs seized. His skin was darker than she'd thought it would be, sun kissed and warm looking in the candlelit room. Her eyes devoured him, took their fill as he stood still and unmoving at the door.

Corded muscles flexed as he stepped toward the bed, his breeches the only article on his person and she remembered to breathe lest she gasp.

"Are you ready?" he asked, his tone business-like and cold. It wasn't a tone she wanted to hear and Louise steeled herself to change his mind about them, about their marriage. Although she was unsure why he pushed her away—the idea of a family and life—she would find out the reasons and she would battle against his walls.

This was their life now whether they wished it or not and she would do everything in her power to make it as best as could be. There may never be love between them, but there would be respect and affection.

She would have nothing less.

$\mathcal{L}$uke bit back the curse upon seeing Louise lying in wait upon her bed. Her large eyes ran over him and he stilled, feeling her inspection of him as if her fingers had slid over his body. Touching every ounce of his flesh.

He strode over to her with a determined stride that was by far the opposite of how he was feeling. Louise was a pretty little thing, and tempted him to take his time with her, to touch, and kiss, taste and explore more than he'd planned.

But no. He would not. Such a path would only lead to pain and he'd suffered enough of that emotion to last him two lifetimes.

The candle beside the bed flickered and he reached out, snuffing it with his thumb and forefinger. The fire bathed the room in golden light, and since this was Louise's first time with a man, the shadows may help in relaxing her. Not to mention, the less he could see of her the better for him.

He leaned down and, taking her face in his hands, kissed her. He wasn't a brute after all, and he didn't want her to suffer any more pain than was necessary. And yet, the moment his lips touched hers he'd known it for the mistake it was.

Her mouth mimicked his and shot fire through his blood. Her hands, tentative at first, but then more bold slid up his chest to clasp his shoulders. Luke came over her, pinning her onto the bed and kissed her deeper still. Slid his tongue into her mouth and lost himself for a moment to the sweet taste that was his wife.

He'd silently hoped she would've balked at his touch. Demand that she wasn't ready and that he should leave. His head spun at her soft, needy gasp and returned kisses. She wanted this. She wanted him. More than he'd bargained for.

The softness of her breasts brushed his naked chest, and frustration rode him. He needed to feel her skin. Taste and savor it for this one night. He clasped the hem of her nightdress, sliding it up her body. She sat up a little as he wrenched it over her head, breaking the kiss only a moment as he came back down onto her.

This was not what was supposed to happen. She was not supposed to respond to him. *He was not supposed to respond to her...*

Luke groaned, giving up his fight against his own desire for the woman beneath him. One night of mutual pleasure would satisfy his duty to her as her husband. After that, they could continue as husband and wife in name only.

His response to her was the same as all his responses to women whom he lay with. A small voice mocked him on his thought.

No it was not.

✦

Louise kissed her husband back with as much passion as she knew how. Her fingers dug into his shoulders, slipping around to clasp his nape, hold him against her as he continued to kiss her as if she were the only woman in the world he wanted.

It was a sweet dream, and one she wasn't silly enough to believe. Not yet at least. But she would change his mind about them. A marriage, even if the couple did not come together in the traditional way, still stood a chance of happiness.

Surely he must see that.

They were certainly getting along well enough in this area if she were to think so boldly. Louise gasped, pushing herself into his hands as his palm molded her breast, his finger sliding over her nipple and spiking liquid heat to pool at her core.

Oh yes, she liked that very much.

Never before had she thought being with a man in such a way could be this intoxicating. His clever touch made her shivery and achy in places she'd not known could shiver and ache and it only left her wanting more.

Even her nakedness did not frighten her as she thought it would. His hand slid down her ribs, across her stomach and then lower still. With a wantonness borne out of years of yearning for what so many about her had—a husband, a lover—she parted her legs and let him touch her where she ached most.

His fingers slid over her most private of places and she moaned, pushing and lifting herself against him. Her body shook, a kaleidoscope of feeling and over-sensitized nerves that longed for something just out of her grasp. He teased her toward it, led her near and then took it away and she wanted it back. Craved it like a bee craves nectar.

"Luke," she gasped as he slid a finger into her body. She should be shocked at her response to him, but how could she be when it felt so right? So delicious, warm and tempting.

His kisses, hot and wet skimmed her cheek, her neck until he reached her shoulder. "You're so tight, Louise," he whispered against her neck, the warmth of his breath teasing her further until she wasn't sure what to do with herself.

"I want you," she admitted. For years she'd watched the gentlemen of the ton from afar, longing to be the woman they asked to dance, to court and flirt with. Instead, she'd been the invisible lady's companion, a wallflower never to be plucked.

Not anymore.

Of course to have fallen into marriage with him had not been ideal, his dislike of her was palpable at times, but now that she was married to him, she would seize the opportunity to make him see her finally.

See past his lofty title to the woman he married. Make him see that although she was common, without any monetary value for his family, she was priceless, just as anyone was, no matter their background.

The security marrying the marquess had given her and her family was a gift she'd not thought to ever have. And she would not squander it. She would nurture and protect it as much as she could. Try and regain their lives without living under the possibility of poverty if something disastrous happened. Give her siblings the stable future they'd always deserved.

Luke moved and settled between her legs, lifting one to rest about his hip. He rocked against her, her core embarrassingly wet and throbbing. She mewled in protest when he removed his hand from there and replaced it with his body. The rigid mass of his penis pressing against her brought forth another new and delicious need to coil through her blood.

Louise lifted her other leg, hooking them both about his back. He groaned and seized her mouth in a punishing kiss, his hands fumbling between them and ripping at his breeches.

And then he was pushing into her. Breaching her body and conquering her as was his right. As was her wish. A stinging pain, quick and sharp, took place as he moved into her and then there was only pleasure. Delicious, wonderful pleasure.

He rocked into her, filling her and pushing her toward more of what she craved. With each stroke he hit some special little nubbin inside of her that ached and longed for more. Louise ground herself against him, wanting more, quicker, deeper, faster.

"Damn, Louise," he growled against her lips. "So good," he gasped.

She clung to him, their movements frantic and hard. Her fingers scored down his back, helping him to take her, wanting him to finish whatever it was that he was doing to her.

And then it happened. Her core convulsed into spasm after spasm of pleasure. Louise cried out, throwing her head back against the bedding and arched her back, allowing the marvelous feelings he evoked in her to overcome her senses, fill and enflame her.

Luke stilled above her, her name spilling from his lips before he pulled out. He pumped his shaft upon her stomach and she watched, entranced, at his body's reaction to her.

Louise lay back onto the bed, spent and satisfied, her bones like liquid beneath her skin.

He came to lay beside her, his face turned toward hers and she reached out, unable not to touch him. Would it always be like this between them? She never knew couples could find such pleasure, and now that she'd tasted what Luke could do to her, well, it left her wanting more.

His hand came over hers, holding it against his cheek, before he frowned, removing it. He sat up and slid across the bed, quickly donning his breeches and walking back toward his room.

"You're leaving?" she asked, sitting up, heedless of her nakedness. After what he'd just done to her, how he'd made her feel, she would walk about naked every day so long as he did such a delicious thing again.

Make love to her...

"Goodnight," he said, pausing at the door.

She watched him, hoping he'd turn and look at her. Change his mind and come back and do more of the same. They were married after all. There was nothing wrong with a husband and wife taking pleasure from each other.

Giving and receiving.

He wrenched the door open and quickly stepping through to his room, slammed it shut, the sound of the key turning the bolt home loud in the quiet night.

Louise sighed, a shiver of disappointment stealing over her skin. What they had done was a start, she reminded herself. The first step in moving forward as man and wife. Luke had not wished to marry, and it would take time and patience for her to win him over.

But she would and she would not scuttle off to the country to hide and disappear from his side. No. Being in London would give her the opportunities to show him he could be happy with her. If only he'd allow himself to be.

And he would be. One day.

CHAPTER 10

*O*ver the next week Luke had gone out of his way to avoid Louise. His wife. The demure lady's companion who had turned into a hellion the moment he touched her. He sat at his desk in his room, twisting the quill between his fingers and wondering how the hell he'd lost all control the night they'd consummated the marriage.

The memory of her welcoming body, her bold kiss and reactions to his touch shot heat to his cock. It twitched, ached, and had damn well been quite the nuisance this last week. Whenever he'd smelled jasmine he'd looked to see if she was near.

If he heard her laughter in the halls of his home, he'd wanted to seek her out and see what was so funny.

He was damn well turning into a fool who was being led by a woman. Their nights out on the town had been pleasant, for her at least. He'd merely accompanied her and then done all he could to bury himself in the gentlemen's card games and stay well away from her touch.

The last thing he needed was to dance with her. If he touched her again, there was no chance that it would end with such a simple embrace. He'd be tempted to carry her from the room over his shoulder like a Viking and take her up against a wall somewhere in the house.

The thought of doing just that had him adjusting his seat.

He swore and stood, striding to the window. He clasped the wood surrounds and stared at the manicured grounds, the flowerbeds in full bloom and green, leafy trees. He willed his body to get a damn grip upon itself.

A delectable figure in deep green came into view and his body stilled. Louise kicked off her slippers and walked the few steps off the terrace and onto the lawn. She strolled about the yard, leaning down to smell the lavender and rosemary. He watched her for a moment and jumped when a light knock sounded on his door.

"Come in," he said.

The door opened and Stephen's blond locks popped around the door. "My lord," he said, an anxious tone to his words. "May I come in?"

Luke gestured for him to enter. "Of course, come in, Stephen." Luke sat back at the desk in his room and nodded for the young man to seat himself on the vacant chair across from him.

Louise's brother glanced about the room, taking in the furnishings before glancing back at him. He looked like his sister, more so than Sophie did. Luke smiled, taking pity on the lad who wrung his hands in his lap as if he were in some sort of trouble.

"What can I help you with?" Luke asked.

Stephen settled himself and turned his attention to Luke. "I was hoping, my lord, that you would teach me how to ride a horse. I've never learned before, you see. We did not have the means for such animals. Although Auntie did have a cat, but, well, you know what I mean."

Luke chuckled at his ramblings. "I understand." He leaned

back in his chair, contemplating the request. "Have you ever ridden any horses before?"

The young lad shook his head. "No, never. I've been in a carriage and cart obviously, but I've never ridden a horse. With you married to Louise I don't ever want to let her down or embarrass her, you see, and what brother to a marchioness does not know how to handle a mount?"

"You love your sister?" The young man's face filled with affection or adoration, Luke wasn't sure which, possibly both. The image of his own sweet sister filled his mind and he knew that it was both emotions.

"Sophie and I owe her everything. She was sent away from us when she was only eight years old. If it weren't for her sending money back to Auntie we would've ended up in a poorhouse. She is the kindest, most hard-working woman I know."

Luke rubbed his jaw, thinking over Louise and her unshakable loyalty to those she loved. She certainly loved her siblings and the Duchess of Carlton. Even in a marriage that she did not care for, she was trying her best to please him. Make him happy when she knew he didn't want the union any more than she did.

"No more titles between us. You may call me Luke and I'd be honored to show you how to ride a horse."

The young man brightened and sat up straight. "Thank you, my lord. I mean," he paused, "Luke. Thank you, Luke."

Luke stood, glad of the distraction of Stephen's sister who strolled the gardens still. "Come then. No time like the present to learn. We'll go down to Hyde Park and start today."

Stephen stood, following close on his heels. "Really? Oh, that would be wonderful. Thank you. I'm keen to become the gentleman that Louise always thought me to be."

Luke clapped him on the back, a sense of pride filling him

at being able to help the young man. "You're fifteen, is that correct?" he asked.

"Yes, sixteen in a month or so," he replied, eagerly.

"Well then, we have plenty of time to get you up to speed and fully competent by the time you attend your first Season."

Luke wasn't sure where the thought came from, but having met the young man, his eagerness to learn from him, his gratitude for Luke's help, humbled him. He'd not been given the chance to guide and help his sister, having lost her so young. Hell, he'd never had parents. Only a grandmother who raised him and then promptly passed away when he was old enough to look after himself. Having this young man to guide, to help, was akin to what he imagined having a brother would feel like.

He'd not had a family for twenty years, nor did he wish for one, his opinion on that had not changed, but he could see the draw of it, certainly. To care for people other than yourself was a new occurrence and one to contemplate. What he could say on the matter was that it did not frighten him as much as he thought it would.

And that in itself was scary.

👑

They returned from their ride some hours later and Luke could not remember a time when he'd enjoyed himself more. Dinner would be served soon and they were scheduled to head out to a musical night at Lord and Lady Elliot's home, and yet Luke did not feel the slightest inclination to go.

Stephen had been the best student. He had listened, taken advice, cared for the mount. A few times Luke had caught him petting the mare as if she would break, speaking in soft tones to win the horse's affection.

Luke had watched on, amused by the whole experience and was ashamed that he'd felt annoyance when he'd first heard of their arrival in town. Sometimes he really could be an ass.

"You're back." Louise stood from the settee before the fire in the drawing room upon their arrival, coming over to inspect her brother. No doubt ensuring that Luke had not injured him in any way.

"Did you learn anything, Stephen? Mrs. Ellis said you were going to ask for assistance with your riding. I hope you've studied well today."

"Stephen learned exceptionally well and picked up all that was required on the first lesson." Luke smiled at the boy, nodding his approval.

Stephen's eyes glowed with enthusiasm. "You will teach me more, my lord?"

"Luke, remember?" he said. Louise's gaze shot to his and he knew she was wondering why he was being so familiar with her brother. Luke could not answer that question himself, but what he did know was that he'd never had a more pleasant afternoon in years. Stephen was not a foolish, headstrong boy, quite the opposite in fact. He supposed being brought up poor, he was thankful for anything that came his way. Opportunities would've been limited indeed in Sandbach. "Of course I will. We will ride out again tomorrow if you like," he said, already looking forward to the outing.

"I would love that. Thank you."

Louise stared at him and the pit of his stomach twisted. The more time he spent in her presence the more he liked what he saw. She too was steady of mind, not tarnished by greed and privilege. It was a welcome change from what he was used to.

"May I learn also, my lord?" Sophie asked, turning in her chair to be part of the conversation.

Louise glanced at him, uncertainty flicking within her blue orbs. He didn't like that she was unsure of him in such a way. He may not have wanted a marriage, but he wasn't a total ogre. And after this afternoon with her brother, he had to admit that he'd enjoyed teaching Stephen how to ride a horse. If Sophie wished to learn also, then he would teach her as well.

"Of course you're more than welcome to join us. We'll go after luncheon tomorrow."

Louise watched him a moment and he could not read what she was thinking, although if he were to take a guess, she was thinking of what had happened to the man she married who wanted no part of any of them. Was only too happy to scuttle them away in Kent and leave them there forever.

👑

The following afternoon Louise decided to join Luke and her siblings on their ride to the park. It had been quite some weeks since she'd been on horseback, and she and Mary had always enjoyed such outings before Mary married the duke.

She started toward the mews, her bottle-green riding gown, newly delivered by Madame Devy only yesterday, fit her like a glove. It was everything a well-made and comfortable gown ought to be. Louise could not stop feeling the soft, velvet fabric and she could not remember the last time she'd actually felt attractive.

Their outing today to instruct her siblings how to ride a horse was something she'd not been able to afford as a lady's companion. For all the luxuries that were afforded her in

Mary's home, both before her marriage and afterwards, it did not give her the monetary means to gift horse riding lessons to Stephen and Sophie.

They all had missed out on so much due to their financial situation. Her aunt had done all she could to ensure Louise's funds went as far as they could, but she had to admit that now being married to a marquess, to have unlimited means was a pleasant change.

If she ensured her siblings never had to worry about money, or how to keep a roof over their heads, she was at least grateful in that way that the marquess had stumbled into her room and nearly ruined her.

Using a mounting block, she climbed up onto the back of her mount before they started toward Hyde Park. Louise took the time to watch Luke with her brother and sister. He rode between them, a groom on either side of them as well, keeping a close watch on both her siblings' horses and that no harm would come to them.

He sat well atop his horse, his straight back and ease was obvious to any who looked at him. The saddle seemed like a second home to his lordship. Her siblings gifted him with multiple questions, and never once did he sigh in exasperation or annoyance. Instead, he answered each query with an intelligent and patient reply and she couldn't help but like him a little more.

The park was a hive of activity, and they rode down toward Rotten Row to keep away from the carriages and people strolling the paths of the park.

Luke stopped his mount before the row, instructing her brother and sister to try to trot before them, explaining how to lift from the saddle using their legs and stirrups, to get into sync with the horse's stride. All the while keeping a firm, but not harsh, grip on the reins.

"Thank you for taking the time to teach them. I think you've made my brother a life-long admirer of yours."

The marquess laughed, his eyes bright with amusement as he watched her siblings ride on the sandy track. "I do not mind. In fact, I've quite enjoyed the last two days instructing him. He's an asset to you."

She tore her gaze away from his too-handsome face that only grew in good looks when he smiled. He'd not returned to her bed since he'd consummated the marriage, and when she saw him like he was now, carefree, relaxed and seemingly enjoying himself, she couldn't help but long for him to be her husband in the truest sense.

"They're both so very good. I'm fortunate to have them as my siblings."

He nodded, his eyes clouding somewhat at her words. She held his inspection of her, willing him to think she too could be an asset to him if only he would give her a chance. Let her show him that marriage did not have to be a life sentence of torture and despair.

"Good afternoon, Lord Graham. How very providential to meet you here."

Louise stilled at the sound of Lady Clara's voice and she turned a little to see the young woman riding toward them, a groom following close on her horse's hooves.

Luke bowed a little from his seat and Louise smiled in welcome, no matter her dislike of the woman she would not be rude. She took in the young debutante's riding gown of blue velvet and gold buttons, a small top hat sitting atop her golden curls. She was so very pretty, rich and from a titled family. Everything Lord Graham ought to have married, and here she was, a lady's companion who'd gained the title through nefarious means.

Unease shivered down her spine and she lifted her chin to

try to dispel the doubt running through her. "Hello, Lady Clara. Are you enjoying the park today?" she asked.

Lady Clara glanced at her and dismissed her just as quickly. "Oh, Lady Graham," she said, watching the marquess and not sparing her a moment more of her time. "I did not see you there."

Louise raised her brow, heat scoring her cheeks at the comment.

"Is your eyesight failing you, Lady Clara?" her brother asked, a contemplative tilt to his head as he stopped his horse before the small party.

"No," her ladyship said, staring down her nose at her brother. He merely pursed his lips in thought.

"Oh, I thought the fact that you could not see my sister meant that you may be going blind. She is sitting practically in front of you."

Lady Clara's mouth gaped before she raised her chin. She laughed a tinkling sound that echoed with condescension. "Oh, so you're Miss Grant's brother I've heard about town. I don't believe I've ever met a lady's companion's sibling before. I would certainly not wish to meet my own servants' family. How lowering of one's position."

Her brother glared. "Rudeness is also a form of crassness and can often show a person's true character, not the face they portray to the public."

Sophie chuckled, covering her mouth with her glove to hide her amusement. Louise tore her gaze to the marquess who looked as shocked as she felt.

Lady Clara glared at her brother before she turned back to Luke all smiles and sweetness again. "Tell me, my lord. Where does your new wife hail from, before she worked for the Duchess of Carlton, of course?"

Louise went to answer before Luke had a chance to, but her brother beat her to it.

"Sandbach, in Cheshire. We lived in a cottage with our aunt if you must know, Lady Clara. Are you satisfied now? Have you insulted my family and my sister enough do you think for one afternoon, or would you like to continue your mocking visit on our riding party?"

The young woman gasped, turning her horse roughly about, but not before catching Lord Graham's eye. "Are you going to let that little nobody speak to me in such a way?"

All eyes turned to the marquess and he glanced back at Louise and then her brother. "Apologize to Lady Clara, Stephen. What you said was unkind."

Louise pushed her horse to come between her brother and Lady Clara. "Stephen will not apologize for anything that he said here today. He was just replying to her ladyship's rudeness toward our family. Come, Stephen and Sophie, we shall leave Lord Graham and Lady Clara to catch up on their own. We certainly would not wish to sully their stature in the *ton* with our lowly bloodlines."

Louise turned and her siblings came abreast of her. She took deep, calming breaths and used the anger that thrummed through her veins to stem the tears that threatened. She bit her lip, refusing to give way to emotion. Refused to break over the fact that her husband had not stuck up for them. Had merely sat by and allowed Lady Clara to mock and ridicule her family. *His family.*

But then, he'd not wanted a family, so it ought not surprise her that he would stand idly by and allow such words to be spoken.

She swore and her brother reached over and squeezed her hand.

"I'm sorry, Louise, but I could not allow that woman to treat you in such a way. I suppose that will end my lessons from the marquess."

She patted his hand, her anger not at him but her

husband. At herself for allowing Lady Clara to pick at her as if she were still a companion. She was a marchioness now, and it was not her fault that the young debutante had missed her chance with Lord Graham. If only the little dimwit knew that the night he stumbled into her room, he was in fact supposed to be meeting Lady Scarboro, a widow he'd been rumored to be sleeping with.

The thought made her stomach churn and she could not reach home soon enough. For a day that had started out so well, it had ended terribly. And tonight she was to attend Lord and Lady Conyngham's soirée.

The torture didn't seem to want to end.

CHAPTER 11

The ride to Lord and Lady Conyngham's soirée was a quiet affair. Luke sat across from her, staring out the window, his jaw locked into a hard line, his eyes narrowed in contemplation. He was angry, he all but thrummed with the emotion, and her stomach roiled at the idea that he would yell at her. She hated confrontation, but nor would she allow him or his lofty friends to degrade her when she'd done nothing to deserve it. If anyone deserved a set-down, it was Luke for putting her in this position in the first place.

Thankful upon arriving at the soirée, she easily sought out Mary, the duke nowhere to be seen. It suited Louise perfectly for if she did not speak to someone soon about what had happened at the park this afternoon, she might scream.

Scream at her spineless husband who had taken the side of a venomous spider instead of his wife.

What was wrong with the man?

Mary kissed both her cheeks in welcome and Louise took her first relieved breath for the day. "I'm so happy to see you,

Mary. I need your opinion and I really do not know which way to turn."

Her friend frowned, taking her arm and walking her to a pair of chairs nearby. They sat and Mary took her hand, concern etched on her features. "Of course you may confide in me. I'm here always. You know that."

She nodded, swallowing the lump in her throat. It had wedged there since Luke had sat silent and still on his horse, voiceless when he ought to have said something. "I don't think my marriage to the marquess is going to work. He hates us I'm sure. Thinks we're beneath him, which even I'll admit that we are when it comes to Society's standards… Even so, his actions today have made it almost impossible for me to forgive him."

The duchess's eyes widened and she held her hand tighter. "What did he do, Louise?" she asked. "Surely, it cannot be as bad as this sounds."

Louise shook her head, wishing that were true. "It is bad and I'm at a loss as to what I can do." Louise explained to the duchess what had transpired between them and Lady Clara. Her brother's set-down to her ladyship, which Mary clapped and congratulated him for, and the marquess's response. As for her husband's inability to speak except to censure her brother, well, the duchess had a completely different reaction.

"Well, Lord Graham needs a good set-down and you ought to be the one to give it to him. You're a marchioness now. His wife. How dare he take the side of Lady Clara."

As if speaking of the debutante brought her forth, she stopped before them, smiling as if butter wouldn't melt in her vicious little viperish mouth.

"Your Grace, Lady Graham, so lovely to see you here this evening. You must be pleased to see her ladyship again, your grace. If you have trouble with your gown or need help throughout the night, at least you have your servant close at hand."

The ladies that accompanied Lady Clara giggled at her insult and the duchess stood. Taller than Lady Clara, the young woman had to take a step back and look up at her grace. The duchess laughed. "Oh dear, you're so very funny, but you know who is really laughing, don't you, my dear?" Her voice dripped sarcasm. The young woman not willing to lose an argument merely raised her brow questioningly.

"I'm sure you're more than willing to tell me, your grace."

Louise stood as well, and was happy to see that she too was taller than Lady Clara. At least in that she was the victor.

"Oh I am." The duchess grinned. "You do realize that Lord Graham was never going to marry you, don't you?"

The young woman blanched and her friends' eyes widened, the two glancing at each other, suddenly unsure where this little tête-à-tête was going.

"You would not know such things. Not when she," Lady Clara said, pointing at Louise, "tricked him into coming to her room so he was forced to act the gentleman and marry her."

The duchess smiled at Louise before turning back to the young woman, who like her friends, seemed quite interested to find out the answer. "Oh no, Louise was nothing but innocent in that situation, but the marquess not so much. You're nothing but a little debutante, a girl in his eyes. He may have played with you before the *ton*, but he would never marry you. Not ever." The duchess reached out, patting the young woman's shoulder condescendingly. "Guard your heart in the future. I would hate to hear gossip about you being so very put out at the marquess's marriage. Very cross behavior if I were to give an opinion on the subject."

Louise's stomach churned at the duchess's words. She knew her friend was only trying to set this chit into her place, but by doing so it left her vulnerable to gossip, more so than she already was. Lady Clara's eyes darted between them, but there was no fear in them, only anger and Louise prayed this little incident would not occur again.

"You mock me, your grace. You're not so very much older than myself and it has not escaped my notice that your marriage too eventuated by nefarious means. And you stand there and give me advice. How very amusing you are."

"I think you ought to go," Louise said, clasping Mary's arm when she stilled beside her. "You've said enough to me and my friends today."

Lady Clara raised her brow. "Where is your husband, Lady Graham?" She glanced about the room. "I do not see him near your person. Perhaps I ought to seek him out and demand another apology. Tell your brother that your husband and I are expecting one."

With that she flounced off, her gaggle of friends close on her heels.

The duchess turned to Louise, her eyes burning in temper. "How dare she. How dare Lord Graham. There is only one thing to do for this horrible behavior."

"There is?" Louise asked, at a loss. She'd never been in so many arguments in her life as she had since marrying the marquess. And never had she thought the women of the *ton* would turn against her, blame her for his lordship's behavior.

"If he isn't going to defend you against those who seek to injure you, then you must hurt him in turn. From tonight onward you are to flirt, laugh and be merry as much as you can within our social sphere. I shall help you with this. If the marquess does not want you for himself, then he will see that others do and are not so judgmental. And then we shall see what he will do."

Louise bit her lip, unsure if she had it in her to do such a thing. Of course she'd been told her looks were tolerable by her aunt, but she wasn't a fool to think she was a rare beauty, a diamond of the *ton* such as Lady Clara was.

But if the marquess was not interested in her, perhaps she ought to show him that there were gentlemen who were. He deserved a little payback after his treatment of her family this afternoon. "Very well, we'll try it for a week or so and see what happens."

"Good," the duchess said, leading her into the fray. "Let us begin."

*L*uke wasn't sure what was afoot, but all that he did know was that his wife had become the most fashionable, most sought-after woman in London. After the altercation at the park with Lady Clara, Louise had pulled away from him completely.

No longer did she accompany him with her siblings on their riding lessons. He'd been surprised when her brother had been open to continuing the lessons, and it humbled him a little that he was able to forgive his lapse in sticking up for the boy's family.

He glanced across the room at those who were listening to the famous soprano, Elizabeth Billington. His wife was seated near the front with the Duchess of Carlton whom he'd also noticed was keeping well away from him these days. Her friendship had cooled, and he hated that his error had caused a rift between them all.

What was worse, now his wife attended events without him, going so far as to not even notify him that she was heading out and the talk at his club was that the rogues and libertines had noticed his inattention once again toward her and were sniffing about her skirts.

His eyes narrowed on his wife as she leaned over to the

duchess, saying something before they both chuckled. Lord Stopford sat beside her, up to his old tricks again it would seem. The gentleman's arm sat across the back of his wife's chair and made the blood in Luke's veins simmer.

What did he think he was about, seating himself so close to his wife? He had one of his own at home, why did he not go pay court to her?

Viscount Anson sidled up to him, a wine in his hand. Graham nodded in welcome, before turning his attention back to his wife.

"I should congratulate you in your recent nuptials with the lovely Miss Grant. I must admit to being uncommonly stupid and blind to her loveliness prior to her marriage. You're a lucky man, Graham."

Luke glanced sharply at him. Did the man have a death wish? Not that he'd said anything overly crude, but the implication was there that he'd seen her now and his interest was piqued.

"Thank you," he said, keeping his reply as short as possible. "And how is Lady Anson, may I ask?"

A grin quirked his lordship's lips, but his attention did not move from Louise.

Cad!

"She is well, and Lady Graham is also very beautiful, with a quick wit about her I like. But I suppose you know that already."

Luke ground his teeth. No, he bloody well didn't know that and he ought to be horse-whipped for not getting to know his wife more. But to get to know her meant caring more than he wanted to. Showing an interest when he didn't want to be interested at all. He didn't want a family, one that could be ripped out from under him at any moment. If he kept them all at arm's length, when disaster did strike, as it always did in his estimation, he would not be as devastated as he had been upon losing his mother, father and little sister.

"Of course," he lied. He didn't speak for a moment, annoyed at Lord Anson and himself for his lack of attention when it came to Louise. He should know that she was funny, what made her laugh. What she was interested in. Instead, his fear of growing attached to her had made her a stranger to him.

He would try to make an effort while also keeping guard of his heart. It wasn't impossible to do. He'd never been a man to lose his head over a chit, there was little reason why he would with his wife. One could be present, know all the facets of one's spouse while keeping one's emotions out of the mix. Surely this was possible.

Luke turned his attention back on his wife and stilled when Lord Stopford's thumb brushed her bare shoulder. A red haze dropped over his vision when she didn't make an effort to remove his hand from her person, merely turned to him, talking as if nothing was amiss.

The hell there wasn't anything amiss.

The opera singer came to the end of her song and the gathered crowd clapped, standing and dispersing about the room. Luke didn't move, and Lord Anson moved away, thankfully, to a group of people who actually wanted to talk to him.

His wife turned in his direction, smiling, and he watched as that pretty smile faded when she spotted him. The duchess glanced in his direction also, dismissing him no sooner as she'd spotted him. As for Lord Stopford, he merely grinned, the amusement in his eyes telling Luke all he needed to know about the fiend and what he was up to. It hadn't been the first time his lordship had seduced a fellow peer's wife, but hell would freeze over before he'd allow Louise to be one of them.

He didn't move, simply watched to see what Louise would do and an emotion very similar to relief poured through him when she excused herself and made her way over to him.

As she came nearer, he leaned down and kissed her cheek, unsure where the show of affection came from, but not sorry that he'd done so. She was his wife, and she was under his protection. He ought to remember that more often when troublesome debutantes sought to insult her in front of him and the *ton*.

She glanced at him in surprise before taking his arm and standing beside him. "I did not know you were going to attend tonight. We could've shared a carriage if that were the case."

He placed his hand over hers on his arm, holding it there. "Your maid told me of plans for this evening, and I've always enjoyed a soprano and thought to attend also. We will return home together if you're in agreement."

She nodded, contemplating him and he could only imagine what was going through her mind. What was he up to? Which wasn't much different from his own muddled thoughts. It was no secret that he'd not wanted to marry the woman beside him, or any woman for that matter, but now that he had, well, she was quite lovely, in temperament and looks, and who could not be a little proud to have such a woman on his arm?

"I would like that."

They stood in silence a moment before Luke broached the subject that had been plaguing him for days. "I owe you an apology, Louise."

"You do?"

He wasn't sure if that were a question or answer and he glanced down at her, his lips twitching at the amusement he read in her twinkling blue eyes.

"I do. For not telling Lady Clara the other day in the park to go to Hades. I should never have asked your brother to apologize, and I should have demanded her ladyship leave. It will not happen again." And it would not. Never would he allow another to insult his wife. He'd been a bastard to have allowed it in the first place.

She smiled at him and something in his chest tightened. "Thank you, Luke. And may I say, that from this moment on, we start afresh."

"I would like that also."

The evening passed pleasantly after that, and even the Duchess of Carlton was warmer to him, similar to how it used to be between them prior to his marriage to her friend. Their hosts offered supper for those who wished to stay.

Luke sat with Louise and the Duke and Duchess of Carlton and listened to their escapades during their childhood. That Louise had been sent away to be the duchess's companion at such a young age didn't sit well with Luke. She'd only been a child. Thrown into a world that was unknown to her and without the support of family. Much like himself. A marquess before the age of eight and thrown into a world that no longer housed his parents or sister.

"Did you miss Sandbach when you left? Eight is very young for one to be taken from those they love."

Louise glanced at him, shrugging a little, but in her eyes he could see the pain of that day lingering in the shadows. She may have been accepted well and loved in the duchess's childhood home, but it was still not her family. No matter how much she may have tried to make it so.

"Of course. I was sent away only weeks after mama and papa had passed away. Sophie and Stephen were only babies really, and I will admit to feeling very lost and unwanted for a time by my aunt. I thought that I had done something wrong. But Mary," she said, reaching for her friend's hand, "helped me laugh again, and I'll forever be grateful for that. I did go home when I could to visit my siblings, and I wrote to them every week. I wanted them to know me, you see. To not forget me. I cannot tell you how pleasant, how very satisfying it is that they're with me now. I suppose I have you to thank for that," she said, chuckling a little.

"Me?" he asked? "How so?"

Louise took a sip of her wine, grinning. "Well, if you hadn't stumbled into my room, I would be in York and my siblings would still be in Cheshire."

Heat rose on Luke's cheeks, but despite himself, he found himself laughing. "I suppose I owe you an apology for that lapse as well."

"Apology accepted." She wrapped her arm about his and he didn't pull away from the contact. In fact, he realized with no amount of shock that he liked having her be tactile with him.

He liked her.

Luke watched as their little party continued to talk and laugh. She had the sweetest laugh and smile when animated and happy. He wanted to see more of her in this way. The thought a few weeks ago would've been preposterous, scary even, but all he felt right at this moment was happy.

♛

*L*ouise took Luke's hand as he helped her into the carriage. The blinds had been drawn in the equipage due to the night having a decided chill. Heat bricks had been placed on the floor for them and once they were on their way, it was a cozy place to spend the next few minutes before they reached home.

She pulled her cloak tight about her shoulders, the warmth from the heat brick soothing under her slippers, just as the evening had been also. Tonight Luke had been attentive, amusing and willing to be by her side, act the husband that he now was. After the terrible situation at the park she'd not thought there was much hope for their marriage, but after tonight she wasn't so certain that was the case.

He had tried and that was better than nothing.

He watched her from the seat across from hers, their knees touching every so often with the movement of the carriage. Her mind pulled up memories of the one and only night he'd come to her bed. Of how at least there they had fumbled along very well indeed.

Other parts of her warmed at the thought and glancing at him, his cutting jaw, perfect nose and dark, hungry gaze left her breathless. What was he thinking right at this moment? If it were anything like her own wayward thoughts all she could imagine was what it would be like to be taken in his arms again.

Her week of playing up to the attention gentlemen of their set had bestowed upon her seemed to have worked. Tonight, certainly, Luke had looked like he'd been ready to kill Lord Stopford when he'd seen her with him. That his lordship had played into her little plan of making him jealous, to make him take notice of her, his wife, couldn't have been more perfect if she'd actually asked him to play a part.

"Lord Stopford was very familiar with you this evening."

His deep voice thrummed through her and she met Luke's dark eyes. Lord Stopford was the last person she wished to be speaking about. "Was he? I didn't notice."

His eyes stole over her, and Louise shivered as if he'd physically run his hands over her person. Her body ached to have his touch once more, to have his clever hands trace her breasts, to feel his mouth and tongue.

She shifted on the seat, unable to look away from him.

"I don't want anyone touching you again. You're mine, and I do not share, my lady."

Louise bit her lip, wondering where this change of heart had come from. Only a few weeks ago he'd not wanted a marriage at all. Certainly he'd not wanted her even under the same roof as his lordship. And now he was being all possessive. She could only hope that it would mean he was willing to make their marriage work.

"I did not think you'd mind a caress here or there. There was nothing sinister in it." She was baiting him, she knew it, but she could not help herself. He'd maintained his distance from her for so long, that if he did not show some sort of emotion, she would scream. He guarded his heart like it was cast in iron—an impossible fortress to breach.

"No one touches you."

She scoffed, glancing out the window. "Someone has to. You certainly do not."

The marquess reached out and clasped her arm, hoisting her onto his lap. She sat across his legs, and his arm came about her back, clasping her waist and pinning her against him. "You want to be touched, Louise?"

Heat pooled at her core at his words. She found herself nodding in reply, unable to form words at present. His dark orbs glinted with a promise of something naughty and she bit her lip, wanting more than anything for him to touch her just as he said.

He kept his eyes locked with hers as his hand slid down her leg, clasping the hem of her gown and sliding it up towards her waist. Air kissed her stockinged legs, and she sighed when he pushed her knees apart a little. Still, his hand slid farther up her thigh until he touched her, *there…*

Oh yes, this was what she wanted. She wanted love, to feel wanted and needed. Not only in life, but during these moments as well. Private moments between a married couple. His finger slid over her mons, flicking the little nub with his thumb as his fingers delved farther, stroking and teasing. Louise reached up and clasped his shoulders, turning herself a little in his arms.

"I want you," she gasped as he circled her nubbin. "Please."

👑

*L*uke groaned and kissed her. Hard. Her sweet mouth opened to him and so too did her legs. They lay open, exposing her sweet heat. He pushed two fingers inside her, wanting to see her come apart in his arms. But he didn't want to take her here, he would find his own pleasure when they were home, in bed where he could savor the time alone.

He picked her up and placed her on the seat she'd just vacated. She made a little sound of protest that made his cock as hard as stone. Damn it, when had she become so damn delicious?

He pushed up her skirts, needing to taste her. Have her come apart on his face. She didn't shy away from his actions and it only made his need for her stronger. He kissed his way up her leg, biting her stocking-clad thigh. Her legs slipped over his shoulders, and ripping open her pantalettes he paused at the delectable view of her mons before him.

She was wet and ready and he kissed her there. Her fingers spiked into his hair as she relaxed into his ministrations. Damn she tasted sweet and he laved at her, flicking her little nubbin with practiced perfection.

She mewled, pushing against him and taking her pleasure against his tongue. He ached with need of her, and he contemplated fucking her. Having her here as well as in his bed later tonight.

Luke pushed two fingers into her heat and she gasped,

rocking on his hand and mimicking sex. It was too much and he pulled away, ripping open his front falls. He wrenched her to the edge of the seat and sheathed himself inside of her in one thrust.

A half gasp, half moan escaped them both. He clasped her about her lower back, and the top of the seat, holding her as he pumped into her tight core.

"Damn it, Louise. You'll undo me."

She moaned, a small satisfied smile upon her lips. "Don't stop."

There was little chance of that. He thrust deeper, his need overriding the fact he was taking his wife in the back of a carriage, like a common strumpet, and yet never had it ever felt so right. He wanted to bring her pleasure, to be the only one who did, today and every day going forward.

She clutched at his hips, her eyes bright with need. He knew the feeling well.

"Let go," he said, lifting her a little to go deeper, to stroke her well.

Her eyes widened and she threw her head back as she came apart in his arms. Spasm after spasm clutched and pulled against his cock and he was powerless not to follow her into bliss. He came hard, let her milk him of every last drop of his seed. He took a calming breath as he slid from her, flopping to sit next to her on the squabs.

She curled into his side and he held her close. Her breath was as ragged as his, and he stared at the ceiling of the carriage, wondering where the hell that overwhelming need to make her his, to ensure him she was his and no one else's came from.

That complexity he'd think on another time. Right now, he couldn't think straight if he tried. He glanced down at her flushed face, a satisfied smile upon her lips and he couldn't regret being with her. Couldn't regret that he'd married her.

But what did that all mean? He reached down and adjusted her gown, settling the skirt back about her legs before buttoning up his own breeches. The carriage rocked to a halt before their townhouse and he helped her down, following her into the house.

He needed to think, and yet he couldn't seem to think straight when he was around Louise. There was something about her that disarmed him. Her compassionate nature by far was one of the best things about her, not to mention they rubbed along well enough when alone.

But he didn't want a wife, right? Or perhaps he'd just not met the right woman. Until now.

He followed her up the stairs and instead of letting her go into her room, he pulled her along into his and shut the door on the world. Shut the door on his muddled thoughts and simply allowed himself to be with her. Enjoy her, and push down the fear that if he allowed himself to grow attached to his wife, it would rip his heart out. That she would always be safe.

Alive.

He kissed her hard and tumbled them both onto the bed. No time like the present to lose himself in her and ignore his fears.

Which was starting to be a fear of losing.

Her.

CHAPTER 12

The following morning Louise all but floated down the stairs to the breakfast table. She entered the room, hoping to find Luke breaking his fast. Instead she found it empty of everyone. She turned to a nearby footman. "Where is everyone this morning?"

She sat at the table and requested tea, toast and bacon.

"His lordship along with Miss Sophie and Mr. Stephen have gone for a ride, your ladyship. They said they would be back to join you at breakfast."

Louise took a sip of tea, sighing at its sweetness just as the door opened and the marquess walked in with her siblings. All of them were flushed, hair askew from riding. They looked refreshed and happy and her heart twisted at knowing her siblings were safe and content.

She met the marquess's gaze and her stomach clutched with need. He was so very handsome and he was hers. Hers to have whenever she wanted. The thought made her cheeks burn and she turned back to her toast and bacon, hoping he'd not guessed her wayward thoughts. She was turning into a wanton.

"You're up?" he said, coming to sit at the table to her right. "You look well today, my lady."

Her gaze tore to him. He grinned, ordering coffee before picking up *The Times* beside him. "Sophie and Stephen are becoming quite the riders, Louise. You would be proud of them."

"We are, Louise. I even had a try of cantering today. I didn't fall off, so one would assume that in itself would be quite the accomplishment."

Stephen laughed. "You did bounce about though, Sophie. I thought you would break your poor pony's back a time or two."

Sophie swiped at their brother's arm, laughing. "I confess I need to learn to sit solidly in the saddle, but his lordship said that will come with practice. And I'm determined to be a great horsewoman."

"I'm sure you will be," Luke said, turning the page on his paper and throwing Louise a grin. "We are going to do a turnabout the park this afternoon in the carriage. All of us," he declared.

Sophie clapped, all but bouncing in her chair at the news.

"We are?" Louise asked, wondering at his change of heart. Had he altered his mind about having a wife and was willing to do things with her? To be dedicated to their marriage as she hoped? After last night, hope had bloomed inside her there could be more between them than she first thought. There was little doubt in her mind that when alone, the air all but thrummed with a delicious tension. Surely they could build on that, work to make their marriage one that was satisfying to them both.

"You're my wife. Your siblings are now my responsibility. A ride in the park as a family is not outrageous."

Louise studied Luke a moment as she'd never heard him

use that term before. She reached out and clasped his hand, squeezing it a little. "A ride in the park would be lovely."

Over the next few weeks they did multiple trips to the park, along with the museum, Vauxhall and Richmond Park. Little by little she learned more about her husband, what his likes and dislikes were. They laughed at gossip, and at balls and parties he was always by her side, a protector and husband.

The night he'd put little Lady Clara in her place before Louise had been an exceptionally high point in their relationship.

Louise stood beside Luke at the Cavendish ball, waiting for the waltz that she'd promised to her husband. She held his arm, enjoying the warmth that his person afforded her, being so close. He glanced down at her and she sighed, swallowing the lump wedged in her throat.

Somewhere over the last few weeks she'd fallen utterly in love with the man. They laughed and played through the days, enjoying their newly formed family, going on excursions and Luke had showed them many sights of London she'd never known of. At night they had come together, their passions set free. Not one evening since he'd pulled her into his room after the delicious carriage ride home had she slept in her bed. Always in his, always waking up in a tangle of arms and legs.

It was heavenly and she'd been powerless to stop her heart from tumbling head first into love with him. She loved him more than she ever thought a person could be loved. He was everything to her. The question was, did he love her in return?

"You look beautiful tonight, my lady," he said, leaning down, his whispered words against her ear sending a shiver of delight down her spine.

"You look good enough to eat, my lord," she teased. His

eyes burned with desire and she clutched his arm harder, liking the fact that the action pushed her breast, her nipple against him and teased her.

"And you wish to eat me here, my lady?" He started moving them toward a nearby door. Louise grinned, following without question.

"Are you not going to dance with me?" she asked, as the first strains of the waltz sounded.

"No, we have other dances to take part in." Luke pulled her through multiple rooms, all deserted and closed off for the ball.

"You know this house very well," she stated, not totally at ease by the fact.

He chuckled. "I've known the family all my life and therefore the house as well. There is nothing more to it than that." He pulled her into a small room moderately furnished. The curtains were drawn, but with a moonlit night, the glow seeped through the fabric and bathed the room in enough light so that they could see.

Luke clasped her hand, walking her slowly to a nearby settee. He sat, looking up at her, and she didn't move. He was so very handsome, with his superfine suit, his groomed hair and perfectly tied cravat. She wanted to muss him all over. Send him spiraling into mayhem as much as he always did to her.

Louise kneeled before him, and his eyes widened.

"What are you doing?" he asked, although not in the least attempting to shift her from her knees.

She reached out and, holding his gaze, slipped free each button on his breeches. His eyes burned with need and heat pooled at her core. Who knew that giving pleasure, which she was utterly about to try, could give pleasure in turn?

"I've wanted to attempt this for some time now. Let me,"

she said, reaching between the flap of his breeches and clasping his rigid member.

He leaned back on the settee, a willing participant, and wickedness thrummed through her veins. Louise pushed his knees farther apart and shuffled closer to the settee. She ran her hand up his thighs, the strong, corded muscles beneath her palms flexing at her touch.

"This is very wicked of you, my lady."

"Hmmm," she said, pulling him free. She bit her lip, having never seen his penis so close before, she'd wondered a moment how on earth she took him inside of her with ease. He was so large, so solid and hard and yet the skin about his phallus was the softest thing she'd ever felt. Utterly amazing.

He groaned, pushing into her hand and she looked up and caught his gaze. His breath was ragged and she tightened her grip, pumping his cock a couple of times to tease him more.

"You're a vixen."

Louise leaned over him and kissed the tip of his penis. It jerked at the touch and she smiled, sticking out her tongue a little to lick the droplet of moisture that sat there. He gasped her name, clasping the nape of her neck, but not urging her down, simply accepting whatever she wanted to do to him. And she wanted to do so much.

Licking her lips, she placed them over his manhood, sliding down his engorged penis, running her tongue along the base of his phallus, teasing the vein that ran there. She sucked, increasing her speed when she noticed that doing so only seemed to give him greater pleasure.

He was delicious as she'd always thought he would be.

*L*uke was sure he saw stars. To have Louise on her knees before him, taking him into her mouth and sucking with an expert precision left him speechless. His body thrummed with need, his balls swelled and ached for release. The base side of him wanted to spill in her mouth, and yet he wouldn't. Not here. Not tonight.

He leaned back in the chair, clasping the nape of her neck as she slid up and down over his cock. He wanted to come, he wanted to fuck her in every which way he could. Over the last weeks she'd weakened his defenses and the walls he'd put up about his heart had slowly cracked away.

His chest ached when he spied her about the house, when she laughed he smiled. Silly and odd things such as these happened all the time, and for the first time since he was a boy, he enjoyed the sound of people in his home.

Somehow Louise had shown him what it meant to have a family again. She had brought him into their fold of three and made them a fold of four and his heart had moved.

Unable to take a moment more of her ministrations, he wrenched her onto his lap, grasping at her skirts to lift them to her waist and sheathed himself fully into her tight core.

They moaned in unison before she lifted on him, kissing him as she took her own pleasure upon his cock.

"You feel so good," he said, kissing her back and tasting himself upon her lips.

She mumbled her agreement as she increased her pace, her little mews of satisfaction keeping him from coming too soon. Her core suckled his cock, warm and tempting as sin. She shook in his arms and he knew she was close. She rode him, knew how to bring pleasure to herself when atop him like this and he sat there, holding her and letting her have her fill.

"You're so beautiful," he gasped. Louise murmured his

name against his lips as the first contractions of her climax spiraled through her. Luke let go, allowed her core to drag him along and he moaned her name as his seed shot into her again and again.

He kissed her deep and long, and the final stone about his heart crumbled away and he accepted it for what it was.

He'd fallen in love with his wife.

CHAPTER 13

a letter arrived two days later from a woman who claimed to be nursing their aunt who'd grown ill during her visit to Bath. The woman requested Louise and her siblings come to Sandbach as soon as possible.

Louise set the letter in her lap, looking over to Luke who sat at his desk, watching her.

"Is something the matter?" he asked. He stood, coming over to her. "Who was the letter from?"

Louise handed it to him, before standing and ringing the bell. "We'll have to go straightaway. I'll have the maids pack a valise for each of us."

Luke looked up from the missive, understanding clear in his eyes. "Of course. I'll have a carriage readied for you. I will follow you in a day or two. I have a parliamentary session tomorrow that I cannot miss."

He stood and pulled her into his arms. She wrapped her hands about his back as tears pricked her eyes. Her aunt had been there for all of them for so many years. Upon her marriage, she'd sent some of her pin money to help her with her travels, and her aunt had wasted no time going about England and Scotland on her tours.

That she had fallen ill in Bath and that it did not sound good was so unfair. "Just when she was enjoying herself, having a little time for herself, and this happens."

Luke rubbed her back, kissing her temple and hair. "Maybe it's just a passing virus and she'll soon get better. Before you panic, wait and see what she is like when you get there."

Louise nodded. He was right of course, but her stomach churned at the idea of losing her. She was the last person they had in the world. Their only living blood relative.

"I will try," she said, just as the door opened and a footman entered.

"Ready the traveling coach and have her ladyship's maid pack a valise for her and her siblings. Straightaway," Luke said.

The young footman bowed. "Of course, my lord," he said, closing the door softly behind him.

Luke leaned down and kissed her. "It will all be well. I promise."

She hugged him again, hoping that were so.

👑

The carriage ride to Sandbach was a long and arduous one. They had forgone staying overnight at the Inn at Northampton, and had instead simply changed horses, ate dinner and continued toward Cheshire. Louise stared out the window, the night closing in fast. The inn had given them heated bricks and in this part of England it looked like they had suffered some summer storms, the road muddy with water, laying over it in places.

She glanced back at her siblings, both of them sound

asleep and each of them leaning up against the side of the carriage. She took in their fine clothes, their fuller cheeks and smiled that she'd been able to finally give them security. The chance of a life just a little easier than their prospects were before.

A large crack sounded and Louise clasped the squabs as the carriage tipped alarmingly to one side. The sound of screaming horses and that of her siblings merged with her own as they rolled off the road and down an embankment. Grass and rock broke into the carriage, wood splintered and Louise gasped as something solid smashed into her forehead. The world blurred before her, all of them flying about like dolls being tossed in the air, before everything went quiet and thankfully, peacefully, black.

👑

One week later, Luke sat beside the bed where Louise lay, still and injured after their accident. Having heard of the carriage accident, he had ordered her and her siblings to be moved to Lord Buxton's estate, a friend of his for many years and who was more than willing to help. Luke had demanded his doctor from London travel to them and attend her posthaste.

Unfortunately, Louise would never get to say goodbye to her aunt, who passed away the day of the carriage accident. His heart hurt for her that she would wake and find out such news, news that would break her heart.

He ran a hand over her face, pushing aside a lock of hair that had slipped over her eyes. Her forehead sported a large, deep gash that the doctor had stitched, but it would leave a scar. Possibly leave her with a scar far deeper than the skin.

The doctor had warned them that she may never be of sound mind again.

That she had not woken at all, not even when they had placed smelling salts beneath her nose was not a favorable sign, or so the doctor had stated. Luke spoke to her daily, just as he was told to do, and yet she continued to lay still, not even a flicker of an eyelid or twitch of her finger.

Nothing.

He sat back, running his hand over his jaw as the sight of her brought back a deluge of memories. Of his mother and father, little sister lying on their beds, cold and dead. Never to laugh and smile again.

He couldn't do it again. He should never have allowed himself to care. Nothing good ever came out of caring for others. Louise, lying in this bed, lifeless and pale. Her stillness was the thing that haunted his dreams, a nightmare come true to life. It was not what he'd ever wanted to partake in again.

The door to the room opened and her brother hobbled inside, the walking stick helping him about. He too had been hurt, a severe sprained ankle, multiple cuts and bruises. Surprisingly, Sophie had fared the best of the three. She had sustained cuts and bruises, but had managed to miss most objects that would cause her harm and had been the one who waved down help for her siblings when she'd climbed up the embankment and sought assistance.

The driver was found dead, and the doctor had come to the conclusion he'd had some medical event prior to losing control of the carriage. Both carriage horses had to be put down. When Luke had inspected the carriage at the nearby town, he'd been amazed anyone had survived such an accident.

Thank God they had, but there was a lesson in this for him. He'd let his guard down, let himself feel and care for someone again only to have that possibly ripped from under him. If his life had taught him anything, it should have been that perhaps he wasn't meant to love. Perhaps he wasn't worthy of the emotion.

"Any change, my lord?" Stephen asked, seating himself at the other side of the bed.

"No." Luke stood and strode to the window, needing to see anything other than his wife in such a condition. "I have to return to London. I'm not sure when I'll be back."

Stephen glanced at him, his face ashen. "You cannot leave. Not with Louise in such a state."

His words tore at his conscience and he pushed it away. He'd almost lost this young man as well. A boy on the brink of manhood that he'd grown to care for. To think that all of them could've been torn away, just like his own sweet sister. His stomach churned at the thought. He couldn't do it.

Panic seized him and he leaned against the windowpane for support, breathing deeply lest he cast up his accounts over the Aubusson rug at his feet. If he left now, before she worsened, then he could distance himself from the situation. Allow others to deal with the issue and be done with it. To stay, to see Louise worsen, wither away and die before him was not to be borne. He'd seen enough dead bodies to last him a lifetime, he would not stay and see another. Not if he could help it.

"I must go," he said, unable to meet Louise's brother's disapproving eyes. Yet he didn't need to look at the young man to feel the loathing aimed at his back.

"If you care for my sister at all, even the smallest amount, you will stay. Help us bring her back."

Luke cringed. Damn it, the urge to bolt coursed through him, yet his feet remained lodged firmly on the floor. His mind screaming to leave and another part of him, a part he'd not thought to use ever again ached to stay. To be strong and face the worst head on.

👑

"*L*uke?" Louise fought against the fog that clouded her mind. Her mind was awash with images of her rolling, of flying about in the carriage as they tumbled down the embankment. The sound echoed in her ears and she opened her eyes, wanting to rid herself of it all.

She focused on the ceiling sporting images of cherubs on clouds. She tried to remember where she was heading and why. She took in the four-poster bed and couldn't place it.

Where was she?

"Luke?"

A warm, comforting hand clasped hers and she shut her eyes. "I'm here, Louise."

"Stephen. Sophie? Where are–"

"We're both well, sister," her brother said, taking her other hand and clasping it tight. He leaned over it and she heard the sob that broke through his composure. "We're a little bruised and sore just as yourself, but we will heal."

Relief poured through her like a balm and she couldn't hold back the tears that ran down her face. They survived. That's all that mattered.

"What happened?" she asked, looking to Luke who sat beside her. She reached out and touched his cheek and stilled when he pulled away from her.

"Your driver had a turn, the doctor thinks he may have suffered a heart spasm that killed him. He lost control of the carriage and it toppled down an embankment, taking the horses with it. It's a miracle that any of you survived."

Her head thumped and she reached up, gasping when she felt the bandage on her forehead. "What happened to my face?" She tried to feel the injury, but could not due to all the bandaging.

"Something hit you in the forehead. Possibly a heating

brick from inside the carriage when it toppled over. You were cut very badly and will have a scar," Luke replied, all business-like and cold.

Her brother smiled at her. "You will still be as pretty as ever."

Louise chuckled and then cringed as the action made her head pound. She gasped. "Auntie. We need to go. We're supposed be at her bedside."

"I'm sorry, Louise," her husband cut in, pushing her back down on the bed. "Your auntie passed away the same day of your accident." Remorse tinged his tone. "You've been asleep for a week. There was nothing that could be done."

She clutched at Stephen's hand and her brother held her tight in turn. "We never got to say goodbye to her. After all that she'd done for us."

"You know Auntie was happy for us all, you especially. She's no longer in pain, Louise. The doctor said that he suspected her to be ill for quite some time but never told any of us. She is in a better place now."

Louise tried to allow her brother's words to soothe her, but they did not. They should have been there. They should have held her hand as she passed away.

"Can you give me a minute with his lordship, please, Stephen?"

He nodded, standing. "Of course. I'll tell Sophie you're awake and that she can visit you in a little while."

"Thank you," she said.

Luke turned toward the door. "Stephen, have a missive sent to doctor that her ladyship is awake and that he must come immediately."

"Of course, my lord," he said, closing the door behind him.

Louise leaned forward, needing to sit up more. "Can you please place some cushions behind me? I'm tired of lying down." Luke helped her to sit upright and she sighed in plea-sure at the new position. She needed that above anything else.

"How are you feeling?" He sat back in his chair, watching her, and she frowned, assessing herself from within. "I'm sore and have a headache, but otherwise I feel well enough. I would love a cup of tea."

The marquess stood and rang the bell. "If the doctor approves it, we'll return to London as soon as you're able."

She nodded, unsure how she felt about going back to town. Right at this moment all she longed for was a quiet country setting, away from the bustle of the Season where she may read to her heart's content and explore her new home some more. Take the time to grieve her aunt.

"I'm sorry about the carriage. About all this trouble." She glanced about the room. It was very beautiful and well kept, but it wasn't as nice as her room in town, or her suite at their country estate.

He waved her concerns away. "You have nothing to be sorry about. I'm just sorry that all of this happened. I thought that you may never wake up."

His words were that of a man who had worried and cared over the past few days, and yet his tone remained cold and aloof. A shiver stole down her spine and she couldn't shift it. "Have you been here all this time?" She hoped he had been. To think that he cared enough to be by her side until she woke would surely show that he cared.

"I have, yes, but I must leave today, unfortunately. I have business to attend to in town that cannot wait. Now that you're awake, I feel no reason to dally any longer."

"Can it not wait?" She reached for his hand and this time he pulled it back, linking both in his lap. He glanced down at his fingers, anywhere it would seem but her. What was going on? Prior to her leaving for her auntie's they had been getting along so very well. They had been becoming close, or so she thought. What had changed?

"It cannot. I'm sorry, but I must leave for London tonight."

Louise sat up, clasping the bed as the room spun. "Please don't go, Luke."

He glanced at her but a moment before he stood and started for the door. "I'm sorry, Louise, but I must."

"Luke," she said again as he walked from the room. She stared after the empty space for a long moment. Even when her sister came into the room, gushed and thanked the Lord that she was awake, still she could not concentrate on what her sibling was saying.

Why had Luke left? What could be more important than being together at such a time? She slumped back on the bedding, allowing her sister to fuss over her while her mind whirled in thought.

She would get better and then she would return home. Maybe it was the shock that she'd woken up. Maybe he really did need to return to town and there was no nice way of telling her that he'd have to leave her. Either way, she would be back in London soon enough and then they would talk. All would be well.

She hoped.

CHAPTER 14

*L*ouise had been back in town a month before she'd been well enough to attend a small soirée that the Duchess of Carlton was hosting. Her husband over the last few weeks had gone out of his way to avoid her. No longer did he attend balls and parties with her, and he'd also stopped coming to her room, stating that she wasn't well enough. That she needed rest, not him.

How little did he know.

She did need him and it was Luke whom she wanted. Tonight was a rare treat and he had accompanied her, and she was determined to reach him. Have them return to how they once were, and to have him not be this cold, aloof man he'd become since her accident.

Louise studied him in the carriage as he stared out the window. "I'm so glad that I've been able to come out to Mary's party. Thank you for coming with me."

He threw her a small smile, but that was all. "Of course," he said, looking back out the window. "We could not let them down."

Louise wrung her hands in her lap, not sure what to say

to reach him. "Is everything well, Luke? Since my accident I've hardly seen you."

He raised his brow, but still refused to glance her way. What was going on?

"I'm sorry you're feeling ignored, but as the wife of a marquess, that is sometimes part of the deal I'm afraid."

She frowned, anger replacing the confusion in her veins. "You did not ignore me prior to my accident, in fact we were together most days. What has changed?" He'd been so attentive, loving toward her and her siblings. He'd purchased her brother and sister a new horse each and gifted Louise the family jewels. The man who sat across from her, dismissive and cutting, was not the man she'd fallen in love with.

He shrugged, his countenance one of disinterest. "Nothing has changed."

She shook her head, having heard enough. "That, my lord is utter cow dung," she said, sitting forward. "You've been avoiding me. I only get one-word answers from you. You never come to my room any longer. Have I sprouted snakes out of my skull since the accident? Will you turn to stone if you dare look my way?"

He did look at her then and the shadows that lingered in his gaze sent chills down her spine. "I'm looking at you now."

She shook her head, unable to take much more of his treatment. If this was how he was going to be—hot one moment and as cold as ice the next—she didn't want to be a part of this charade. It was not what she wanted. She wanted him to love her as much as she loved him. That he'd not been there for her during her weeks of recuperation should have warned her to expect less from him.

Foolishly she'd hoped it had merely been a scare he'd suffered and he'd soon be back to rights. Just as she was. Her hopes had been dashed during the weeks she'd been back in town and he'd slowly, gradually disappeared from her life altogether.

"Is this the kind of marriage you want? Do you want to be strangers? A husband and wife in name only? Tell me now, because if that is so I want no part of it."

He scoffed at her words and she flinched. "It is a little late for that, my lady. You married me, did you not? Knowing full well I never wished to be saddled with a wife. This is the price you have to pay to have my name. I'm sorry you feel disappointed, but it is what it is. I suggest you move on and make the best of the bad situation."

Louise nodded, her eyes burned with unshed tears. "I suppose you're right. I will do as you ask."

The muscle at his jaw flexed and he stared at her a long moment, before he moved toward the door as the carriage slowed. "We're here. Come," he said reaching for her hand when he stepped out onto the footpath.

Louise didn't move. "I have a sudden headache. Please give my apologies to Mary and the duke."

He gestured for her to follow him. "Come, Louise. You must attend."

She shook her head, wrapping her cloak about her shoulders, needing its warmth after the sudden chill running through her veins. "No. Please notify the driver to return me home. Thank you."

He closed the carriage door, the muscle in his jaw flexing, before he said, "Return Lady Graham home, thank you," he said to the driver and without a backward glance, started for the townhouse doors. Louise sat back in the squabs, rubbing her thumping forehead. "Goodbye, Luke," she whispered as he disappeared from view just as the carriage lurched forward and they went in their different directions.

To start different lives.

CHAPTER 15

*L*ouise sat on an outdoor reclining chair, a woolen blanket about her knees as she looked out on the grounds of her home. Or Lord Graham's estate in Kent at least.

She'd been here several weeks now, and still he'd not come. She'd hoped when he'd found her gone from their London home after the duke and duchess' soirée that he would've come to his senses and followed her.

He had not and now, out of pure stubbornness, she would not return to town and seek him out. She'd asked for him to tell her what was wrong. Asked him to return to the way they were, and instead of explaining his actions, he'd thrown at her coldness, aloofness. Dismissed her wants and needs and instead demanded a marriage like the one he'd wanted prior to growing close to her.

But what about what she wanted in a marriage? Did he not care for her feelings at all?

Sophie sat on the chair beside her, laying a book on her lap as she stared out on the lawns. "I saw that the mail had come today. Anything from the marquess?" her sister asked, opening her book to where she'd finished reading last.

Louise shook her head. "Only a letter from Mary and Auntie's solicitor. The cottage in Sandbach has been sold and the funds are being placed into investments to hopefully give you and Stephen some funds upon your marriage."

Sophie reached out her hand, clasping hers. "You're always so good to us. Thank you for caring for us so very much. You are the best sister anyone could ever wish for."

Louise patted her hand, fighting back tears. She'd been crying a lot lately, and at the oddest things. Not to mention her stomach had been very unstable. The two facts ought to bring her joy for she knew what they meant, but they did not. Not as it should in any case.

She wanted to share her news with her husband, with her siblings, but she could not. Not yet at least. When she had control of her emotions, had closed her heart off from the man she'd married who had made it abundantly clear that he cared very little for her, then she would tell him and her family.

She clutched at her stomach. No matter what happened between her and the marquess she would love this child with all her heart. Never allow the child to feel unwanted or unloved as she was feeling right at this moment. Stupid of her to be so attached to a man who had told her he'd never wanted to marry her, but her heart had other ideas and she'd been powerless to not fall heedlessly in love with him.

Little good that did for her.

"Are you going to tell the marquess?"

Louise glanced sharply at her sister, frowning. "What do you mean?" she asked, hoping she meant something entirely different.

Sophie gestured toward her stomach. "The baby? Are you going to tell him about the baby?"

Louise took a calming breath, her stomach roiling in dread. "How did you know?"

Her sister scoffed, picking up her book. "You vomit each morning, sleep in the middle of the day and cry when you lose at chess. I think it's pretty obvious that you're pregnant."

At her sister's words she laughed, the first time in an age and she could not regret her amusement. She'd not found many things funny these past few weeks, but somehow her brother and sister always managed to cheer her up.

"Does he deserve to know?" she said, regretting her words as soon as she'd said them. Of course he deserved to know, but did he want to? The thought that he would scorn their child as much as he'd scorned her filled her with panic and not a small amount of anger. She would not allow him to treat their child such. Over her dead body would she allow him to disregard their son or daughter.

"You need to tell him, Louise." Her sister sighed, shaking her head. "His actions of late make no sense. When you were injured, he was beside your bed every day and night. Refused to leave the room unless forced. For him to up and leave, almost panic when you woke makes no sense."

Louise frowned, thinking on her sister's observations. "I asked him in London what was troubling him and he would not say. He was so cold and aloof, very disinterested in me and so very different than how he was prior to my accident."

Their brother came out on the terrace, only a small limp remaining from his injured ankle. "I think I know what happened to the marquess."

"You do?" both Louise and Sophie said in unison. "What?" Louise asked.

"He never told me exactly what occurred, but he did lose his family when he was young, right?"

Louise nodded. "That's right. He wasn't with them when the accident occurred, and he'd been orphaned."

Her brother nodded, a contemplative look on his face. "It was a carriage accident, wasn't it? I'm sure I heard the staff at Lord Buxton's estate talking about it. They mentioned how very unlucky the marquess was that he'd almost lost his wife and her family in the same way he'd lost his own."

Louise stared at her siblings in shock. How had she not realized that fact herself? She thought back over everything she'd known of the marquess, before and after their marriage and although she'd known of his family's death, she'd never asked him how it had occurred.

A carriage accident.

Poor Luke. Her own accident had no doubt brought forth terrible memories and fears he'd sooner forget and so instead of holding her close, being thankful for her survival, he'd pushed her away.

He'd protected his heart.

"I have to return to London." At her words a footman stepped out onto the terrace. "My lady, the Marquess Graham has arrived."

CHAPTER 16

A month after Louise had left London Luke had crumbled and gone to Whites, unwilling to stay at home another day. He'd declined all invitations to events about town, and had instead thrown himself into estate business, going so far as to visit his estates in Sussex and Cornwall. All the while he knew that Louise was staying at Ashby House in Kent. He'd fought with himself not to go to her. To beg for forgiveness. For her to understand.

But what would he say? There was not a lot he could say to fix the error that he'd made, but how?

The leather chair crunched across from him and he glanced up to see Carlton sitting before him. A glass of brandy swirling in his friend's hands.

"We've now turned to drinking, have we?"

Luke feigned ignorance and took another sip, his head spinning a little since he'd had many a glass before this one. "I don't know what you mean."

The duke raised a disbelieving brow. "Why don't you just admit that you miss her, you stubborn fool?"

He leaned farther back in his chair, feeling less than

inclined to listen to reason when spoken to in such a way. But then what did he expect? He'd acted an ass and the duke knew it. Hell, all of London knew it.

"I doubt she'll want to speak to me even if I did seek her out. She left me, remember?"

The duke scoffed. "You forced her hand. What did you expect? I saw the way you watched her at balls and parties after her accident. You love her and yet you pushed her aside. You need to go to Kent and fix this problem you've created. You need to tell her you love her and that you're sorry for being scared."

Luke placed his empty glass on the table before him, running a hand over his jaw, surprised to feel stubble there. Hell, he'd let a lot of things slide over the last few weeks. Even his own appearance.

Carlton was right. He was scared. Scared to death of loving Louise so fiercely that the thought of losing her chilled his soul. But he could no longer live with that fear. He'd let it control him long enough, taint his life and haunt his dreams.

He swore and stood. "I leave early tomorrow morning." The decision lifted a weight that had been pressing on his shoulders for years and with it he felt free. No longer would he live a half life. Now was time to live. It would be what his parents wished. What little Isabella would want for her big brother.

The duke stood, draping his arm about his shoulders and walking him toward the upstairs smoking room doors. "Good man. Give our love to Louise and good luck, my friend, even though I'm sure you will not need it."

He nodded, hoping that were true. "See you next Season."

Luke left Whites and made his way home, giving orders upon his arrival of his intention to leave first thing in the morning to Ashby House. His staff went straight to work in preparing for his departure. Luke headed upstairs, needing to work on his own hygiene before he saw Louise again. His world had turned to shite, along with his appearance, but he didn't need her to see it also. He would hide that from her at least outwardly, for heavens knew, he was a mess inside and his only cure was his wife.

Louise.

CHAPTER 17

*L*uke handed the footman his missive to give to the marchioness and started toward the old elm tree that overlooked the valley on the western side of the estate. He stared down at his parents' graves, and his little sister's. Forever young at only six years of age.

He shut his eyes a moment, stemming his tears before he looked down at the three headstones, always the same emotion washing over him when he visited them.

Guilt.

Guilt that he'd refused to go on the outing that day. He'd wanted to stay at the estate and play with his toy soldiers. He'd always wondered if he'd been there that maybe he could have saved her. Maybe being in the carriage may have changed all their fates.

A twig snapped behind him and he turned to find Louise standing before him. She was the sweetest thing that had ever come into his life. A woman so full of love that she'd wanted to give it to him too, even when he'd not wanted a bar of it. Still she persisted and eventually had worn him down. Won his heart.

Only for him to turn her away at the first sign of difficulty. He was an ass, but hopefully, she would forgive him his stupidity.

"Louise, this is my family," he said, stepping aside and showing her the graves beyond.

She walked past him, kneeling to read each one, before she stood, her dark-blue eyes full of questions and hurt. Damn it. He'd put that emotion there and he ought to be horsewhipped for doing so. He'd never wanted to hurt her. Not intentionally.

"They died when I was eight. Heading for a picnic in which I refused to go on. I didn't want to leave my toys, you see, and so being the selfish little ass that I was, I got to play with my toys while they died not two miles from here."

"Oh, no, Luke." She reached out to him, taking his hand. He shook his head at her ability to care, even after all he'd done to her. He played with her fingers a moment, needing the time to compose himself, the lump in his throat awfully large.

"The horses were spooked and the carriage rolled. They all died and they never returned home that night. The house was shut up and I was bundled away to Sussex to live with my grandmother. A woman who tolerated me, taught me how to be a marquess, but little else. I forgot, you see."

Her eyes held his and he could see the unshed tears in her eyes. "What did you forget, Luke?" she asked.

"I forgot what it was like to have a family. A caring and a joyful family to come home to. I forgot what it was like to be responsible for others and care for them. To want the best for them now and for their future." He stepped closer to her, taking both her hands. "When you were hurt I couldn't see straight. The fear that you would never wake up, just as my family had never woken up...I couldn't do that again and I panicked because I'd already gone too far."

"Too far?" She frowned, stepping closer. "How?"

He glanced at the sky, praying for strength lest he lose his composure completely. "I love you, you see. The thought that I would lose you, that you could be taken away from me within a moment of time. I couldn't stand the thought."

She reached up, clasping his jaw. "So you pushed me away to protect yourself." Louise lifted herself and wrapped her arms about his neck, holding him close. "I'm here, Luke. I didn't die. I survived. This time, you didn't lose everything."

He wrapped his arms about her back, feeling the warmth of her skin, her scent of jasmine, the expansion of her chest with each breath she took. So unlike his family who had been cold, gray, and still as death.

He clutched at her, the memory bombarding him and he gasped, and for the first time since he was a child, he cried. Cried for the loss of his parents, for the loss of a sister who had so much to give to the world and had never had the chance. For the loss of his childhood and his ability to love. But not anymore. Louise had broken down his walls, had showed him that to love was to live and he wanted nothing more than to love and be with her forever and a day.

"I'm so sorry, my darling," he said, kissing her neck. "I will never push you away again. Ever."

Louise rubbed his back, a comforting gesture that he remembered from his own mother. "I'm sorry too. I didn't know, Luke and I should have asked. When we lost our parents, we were thrown into our auntie's home, and although she loved us, we were so poor. I too was sent away at eight, but having my siblings to love and care for made me only want to protect them, keep them safe always."

She paused, pulling back to look at him. "I intended to travel to York for work, but I did hope to marry one day to a man I loved who could support me and my siblings. When you stumbled into my room that night I thought all of my dreams had been crushed. That you had ripped that future away from me, but you had not. You only made my dreams come true."

She reached up, rubbing away the tears drying on his cheeks.

"I did?"

She nodded. "You did." She smiled, leaning up to kiss him. "I love you too and I promise, it will take a lot more than a carriage accident to tear me away from you. You have my word on that."

He tried to smile, but his lips merely wobbled. "Promise?"

She wrapped her arms about him again. "I promise."

EPILOGUE

Seven months later

Louise pushed as pain ripped through her body, threatening to tear her in two. The midwife kneeled between her legs, telling her to push, that she could see the baby's head, but she'd had enough. She just wanted it all to end. For the pain to stop.

She tried to close her legs and the midwife *tsked tsked* her, pushing her knees apart. "Come on, my lady. Push hard. We're nearly there."

Luke lifted her higher on his chest and held her hands. "Come, my love. Push as hard as you can. We're almost there."

A baby cried in the hands of Sophie who stood beside the bed, her sister's tears dripping onto the newly born babe and Louise wanted to tell her to stop dribbling on the baby, before another contraction hit and she bore down. The only time she felt a little relief was when she pushed.

"That's it, my lady." Louise flopped back on Luke, panting.

"The head is out now, my lady. One more push for the shoulders and we'll be there."

"It better be so," Louise said, ignoring Luke's chuckle at her ear. The contraction came fast and hard and she pushed with all her might, wanting the child out and the pain finished.

Please, God, let it be done.

She screamed as the babe pushed through and out into the world, its squeaking cry loud in the room, starting off the other baby her sister held.

"It's a boy, my lord, my lady. You have both a girl and boy."

Luke shook behind her and she patted his arms, knowing that her husband was emotional over the news. The midwife handed off the child to her maid and Louise looked back at Luke, smiling. He leaned down, kissing her softly. "Thank you, my darling for giving me such a wonderful gift." He glanced up at the babies, pride overflowing from him and making her smile. "I cannot believe it. Twins."

"Well, they do run in the family, need I remind you, Luke," her sister said, pointing at herself.

Louise laughed and the midwife declared her well enough to lay back on the bed. Luke moved from behind her and helped settle her on a bed of pillows at her back and then she gestured for the babies to be handed to them.

Sophie placed the little girl in Louise's arms and Luke, having taken their boy from the maid, came to sit on the bed beside her. They stared and played with the babies for a time as the midwife went about cleaning the room and giving instructions to the staff.

"I shall be back after dinner and will sleep here this evening, just to be sure all is well through the night."

Luke glanced up and nodded. "Thank you, Mrs. Turner. That is most welcome."

Sophie walked the midwife to the door. "We'll leave you alone for a little while. I'll bring Stephen in a little bit to meet his new nephew and niece."

"Thank you, Sophie for today. You were wonderful." Her sister nodded and left, closing the door softy behind her.

Louise looked between the babies, sweet and innocent and her heart filled even more than she'd ever thought it possible. "We have a little family," she said, running her finger over her daughter's golden hair that was only just visible atop her head.

Luke leaned over and kissed Louise on the temple. "We were already a family, now we're merely a bigger one."

She chuckled, supposing that were true. Her son fussed in his father's arms and Luke cooed to him and he soon settled again. "He likes you." Louise reached out and touched her son's cheek, so soft and new. So perfect.

"May I ask something of you, darling?" Luke met her gaze, before looking down at his daughter.

"Of course, anything."

He took a breath, quiet a moment before he said, "I would like to name her after my sister. I think Isabella suits her pretty little face."

Louise looked back at her daughter, nodding. "I think she looks like an Isabella as well." She lifted her daughter, kissing her cheek. "Hello, Isabella. It's lovely to meet you."

Luke lifted their son and kissed him in turn. "And what about this strapping young man? What shall we call him?"

"How about we name him after his father. I've always had a love for that name."

Luke glanced at her quickly. "After me?"

Louise nodded, turning back to her son, not quite believing she'd just given birth to two babies and had lived to name them at all. Certainly, throughout the ordeal there were times where she'd thought she would absolutely die.

"Yes, after you. Luke, Viscount Tomlinson, future Marquess Graham. I think it suits him very well."

Luke caught her gaze, and she read all the love that he had for them in his eyes, for they no doubt matched hers. He leaned down and kissed her again, lingering a little this time. "Thank you, my darling. Have I said today how much I love you?"

She grinned, nodding. "You have. Multiple times, but you may say it again if you want. I like hearing it."

"I love you. I love you. I love you," he repeated.

She chuckled. "And I adore you too."

Forever.

Dear Reader,

Thank you for taking the time to read *A Midsummer Kiss*! I hope you enjoyed the first book in my Kiss the Wallflower series. Louise and Luke didn't have the smoothest time getting to their happy ever after, but thankfully they made it in the end. I hope you enjoyed Luke and Louise's journey towards love.

I'm forever grateful to my readers, so if you're able, I would appreciate an honest review of *A Midsummer Kiss*. As they say, feed an author, leave a review!

If you'd like to learn about book two in my Kiss the Wallflower series, *A Kiss at Mistletoe*, please read on. I have included chapter one for your reading pleasure.

Tamara Gill

A KISS AT MISTLETOE

KISS THE WALLFLOWER, BOOK 2

Lady Mary Dalton fills her time with anything she pleases—and she pleases to do as she likes. With no interest in a husband, Lady Mary is perfectly content to remain in Derbyshire for the rest of her days. However, Mary's parents have other ideas.

. . .

For the Christmas festivities at Bran Manor, Mary's brother brings home the Duke of Carlton, an infamous man known for his many improprieties, as well as for his distaste in matrimony. Despite his rakish ways, Mary is drawn to him in the most vexing and exasperating way.

But when Mary stumbles into the Duke of Carlton's arms one snowy eve, an undeniable attraction is set into motion. Suddenly, marriage no longer seems so horrific–for either of them.

CHAPTER 1

*L*ady Mary Dalton, eldest daughter to the Earl of Lancaster jiggled her fishing pole, having felt a rapid jerk of her line. Too slow to catch the fish, she left her line in the water hoping to feel another little nibble and possibly reel in a nice-sized carp or bream for Cook to prepare for dinner tomorrow.

The snow relentlessly fell outside as she sat wrapped up in furs and wool on the family's frozen lake in Derbyshire. The ice house her father had the servants move onto the lake each year was a welcome retreat from her mother's complaints. Mama didn't think ladies should fish, particularly in the middle of winter. Women should be wives. Women should have husbands. Women should have children. Her daughter should be married by now…

Blah, blah, blah, she'd heard the words too many times to count.

It was practically the countess's motto. Unfortunately, what her mama wished for was the opposite of what Mary wanted. She'd never been like her friends, had never loved shopping in London in the weeks leading up to their first

Season. She cared very little if the men of the *ton* thought her a worthy, profitable or pretty ornament for their arm.

The outdoors had always been her passion and some days she'd wished she'd been born a man, or even into a family that were not titled and rich. Just an ordinary, working family that could do as they pleased. At least, that was what she'd always thought everyone else had since her own life had been so orchestrated.

Mary jiggled her line a little and sighed. At least she was home at present, thanks to her mama falling ill with a cold that she could not possibly stay in Town to endure since someone might see her red nose.

With any luck, her mother would decide to stay in Derbyshire and not travel back to Town to finish up the Little Season before Christmas. Thankfully, spring and summer would soon return and she was looking forward to those months. When the snow melted away and rivers ran and she was able to go outdoors again not just to fish on the ice but to walk the surrounding hills and forests and climb the rocky outcrops that scattered her magnificent county.

The door to the icebox opened and her father entered. He was rugged up in a fur coat, a hood covered his head and most of his brow. A thick woolen scarf wrapped about his mouth and nose, and he looked like an Eskimo. Mary chuckled as he came in and shut the door, before sitting on the little wooden stool across from her. He picked up the spare fishing rod, placing bait on the small hook and dropped the line into the water, dangling it just as she had.

"Mary, there is something we need to discuss, my dear," he said.

His downcast tone didn't bode well for them to remain in the country and she prepared herself for the disappointing news that was undoubtedly to come.

"My dearest girl is to be three and twenty in few days, and

it is time for us to have you settled and married before the end of the next Season. We thought our annual Mistletoe Ball would be the perfect opportunity to invite our neighbors and their guests to celebrate Yuletide. It would also act as a reintroduction for you into society and to show those present that you're most definitely seeking a husband next year and are open to courtship."

The thought sent revulsion through her and she stared at her father a moment, wondering if he'd lost his mind. It was one thing to return to London, but using their Christmas ball as a means to showcase her assets was mortifying. "Must we go back to London at all? You know I do not do well in Town. I am not like the other girls. I don't take pleasure in grand balls and parties. I'm much more comfortable here in my ice fishing box, swimming in our lake or walking the beautiful park with Louise. I'll be miserable if you make me endure another Season. Even you said how much you loathe London and the backstabbing *ton* who live there."

Her father half laughed, jiggling his line. "You're right I do abhor it, but you need a husband, to be given a secure future and happy marriage. Just as your mama and I have had."

That was true, her parents had a very happy and loving relationship, but that didn't mean such a path was the one she wanted to tread. What was wrong with being a wallflower that wilted into an old, unmarried maid? Nothing in Mary's estimation. To be married meant she would have to conform to society, be a lady all the time, host teas and balls. Live in Town most of the year and submit to a husband's whims. Such a life would not be so bad if she found a man to marry whom she loved, and who loved her. A gentleman who liked the country life over that of London and allowed her the freedom which she was used to. But after numerous failed Seasons already, *that* was unlikely to occur.

Her heart twisted in her chest. "I do not want to return. Please don't make me, Papa."

"We must, but with Christmas upon us, we'll have more time here at Bran Manor, plenty of time for you to enjoy the last few months of being an unmarried woman."

Her father looked at her as if such news would make everything well. It did not.

He cleared his throat. "We want to see you happily married and settled. I would love nothing better than to welcome a titled gentleman, worthy of an earl's daughter into our family. You never know, you may find a man who loves the hobbies that you do, admires and appreciates your exuberance for life and country walks."

Or she might find no one of the kind, make a terrible mistake that she would be stuck with for the rest of her life. "What if I don't find anyone with such qualities, Papa? Last Season, certainly I never did. All the gentlemen were self-absorbed dandies who inspected mirrors more than they interacted with the women surrounding them."

Her father chuckled, tugging sharply on his line and pulling out a good-sized trout.

Mary despaired at the sight of his catch. She'd sat here for hours and hadn't caught a thing and here was her papa, not here five minutes and he'd caught the largest fish she'd seen all winter.

She shook her head at him. "You're no longer invited into my ice hut. You cheat," she said jokingly, smiling at her papa.

He grinned, looking down at his catch. "I'll have Cook prepare this for tomorrow night. It will be a feast."

"You know, Papa, I'm an heiress and financially independent no matter whom I marry, thanks to you, Mama, and Grandmother Lancaster. Why should I marry at all? It's not like the family needs funds, and I will never be considered an old, poor maid not worthy of society's company. Your title and wealth prohibit such ostracism. So is it really necessary that we go? There may be a young man in Derbyshire who is looking for a wife and would be perfect for me. I could have the love of my life right beneath my very nose, and miss him by going to London, looking for the wrong man."

Her father paused from putting the fish in a nearby basket, before he said, "I must remember to give your tutor a better letter of recommendation due to the fact you're able to negotiate and barter as well as those in the House of Lords." Her father threw her a consoling smile. "But, alas, we do not live in a time where young women of means and of family can live independently without a husband. I will not allow you to be placed on a shelf to have dust settle on your head, nor will I allow you to live an unfulfilled life without a husband and children of your own. You would be an asset to anyone's family you married into, and I want to see you happy."

Anger thrummed through her at the narrow-minded idea that she needed a man to make all her dreams come true. She did not need a husband to be happy, and the sooner her father and the men hunting her fortune realized this, the better.

Mary yanked up her fishing line, placing her rod against the wall. "I don't see why I have to marry anybody. This is 1800! A new century, please tell me that gentlemen of society and England will come out of the dark ages and see that women are worth more than what they can bring to a marriage, or how large a dowry they have, or how wide their hips are for breeding!"

Her father raised his brow, clearly shocked. "Hush now! I'll hear no more protest from you. I would never force you into a marriage you did not want with your whole heart. We want you to be happy, to find a gentleman who allows you the freedom to which you've grown accustomed. But you *will* marry, my child, and you will continue to have Seasons in Town until you do."

Mary couldn't believe her father. It was as if he were only half listening to her. "I will not find someone. I know this to be true." She crossed her arms, hating the idea of going back to London. "You know as well as anyone that I'm terrible around people. I get nervous at balls and parties so that I'll say something out of line, or not be fashionable enough. I stutter when asked direct questions, and my face tends to turn a terrible, unflattering shade of red during all those things. Please do not do this to me, Papa. *Please*," she begged him.

Her father stood, seemingly having enough fishing for one day. "You are going and for your mother's sake, you will enjoy the Season or at least make a show of enjoyment while in public. Do not fret, my dear," he said, his tone turning cajoling. "We will be there with you. To hold your hand and not let you fail."

She blinked back the tears that threatened. Her first Season had been miserable. Her mother, even with a fortune at her disposal had not procured her a fashionable modiste and so she'd been dressed in frills and ribbons that made her look like a decoration instead of a debutante. Her gowns had clashed against her olive-toned skin and dark hair and not a lot had improved regarding her wardrobe since that time.

Even despite her father being titled, with multiple properties about England and her dowry being more than anyone could spend in two lifetimes, no one had befriended her or took her under their wing other than her dearest companion Louise, of course. Mary sighed, knowing it was not entirely everyone else's fault that she was ostracized in Town. She'd gone above and beyond to distance herself from girls her own age, and had been cold and aloof to the gentlemen who had paid court to her.

At three and twenty, what was left open to her but to be standoffish. To marry at such a young age would mean her lifestyle, her love of the outdoors and pursuits indulged in only by those of the opposite sex would end. Would have to end because her new husband would demand it of her. Demand she acted as the earl's daughter she was born and as his wife.

Mary met her father's gaze and read the concern in his eyes and a little part of her disobedience crumbled. She hated to disappoint her parents, and of course she wanted them to not worry about her, but how could she marry and remain the woman she was?

She narrowed her eyes, thinking of possibilities. "If I'm being forced to go, Papa, and I do wish to state that I am in no way agreeable about traveling to London. But if I do have to go, smile, dance and play the pretty debutante, there are some rules that I wish to instruct you and Mama of."

Her father stopped adjusting his fur coat and gave her his full attention "What is it that you want, Mary? We're open to negotiation."

"I will choose whom I marry. I will not be swayed otherwise. The man I marry will suit me in all ways and I will not be pressured to choose if one does not materialize next Season." Mary raised her chin, waiting for her father's response, but when he did nothing but stare at her patiently, she continued. "I want a new wardrobe for the Season. And I'd like a lady's maid of my own, not Mama's. She has a habit of putting my hair up in styles like Mother's and it makes me look…" Mary fought for words that wouldn't hurt her father's feelings when discussing his wife.

"A woman of mature years?" he said, smiling a little.

"Yes." She nodded empathically, "That is exactly what I mean."

Her father regarded her for a moment before he came

over to her, placing his arm about her shoulder. "That does not seem like it's too much to ask. I will speak to your mama and ensure she will not stand in your way."

"Thank you, Papa." Mary busied herself putting her gloves on while she pushed down the guilt her request brought forth. Had she wanted to, she could've asked for a new modiste and maid years ago and her parents would never have stood in her way. But her determination to remain an unmarried maid had made her hold her tongue. Being unfashionable in Town had meant very few wished to be around her, or be seen on the dance floor with her, and that had suited her very well. But she could not remain so forever, not if her parents were so determined to see her as a wife. If she had to embark on this side of life, at least it would be under her terms and with any luck she'd find a gentleman who'd enjoy the outdoors as much as she did and not wish to clip her wings. To find such a man she supposed she would have to mingle more and actually bother to get to know them this Season.

"Come, let us get this fish back home. I'm sure the dinner gong will sound very soon."

Mary let her father shuffle her out the door, before they started back toward the house. In the dissipating light, the estate was a beacon of warmth and much preferred than where they currently were. Mary resigned herself to the fact that they would return to London in the spring, but at least she would have control of her gowns and there was Christmas here in Derbyshire to enjoy.

Her elder brother always brought friends to stay, and so this year would be just as merry as every other. A little calm before the storm that was the Season.

LORDS OF LONDON SERIES
AVAILABLE NOW!

Dive into these charming historical romances! In this six-book series by Tamara Gill, Darcy seduces a virginal duke, Cecilia's world collides with a roguish marquess, Katherine strikes a deal with an unlucky earl and Lizzy sets out to conquer a very wicked Viscount. These stories plus more adventures in the Lords of London series!

LEAGUE OF UNWEDDABLE GENTLEMEN SERIES AVAILABLE NOW!

Fall into my latest series, where the heroines have to fight for what they want, both regarding their life and love. And where the heroes may be unweddable to begin with, that is until they meet the women who'll change their fate. The League of Unweddable Gentlemen series is available now!

ALSO BY TAMARA GILL

TO VEX A VISCOUNT
TO DARE A DUCHESS
TO MARRY A MARCHIONESS
LORDS OF LONDON - BOOKS 1-3 BUNDLE
LORDS OF LONDON - BOOKS 4-6 BUNDLE

To Marry a Rogue Series
ONLY AN EARL WILL DO
ONLY A DUKE WILL DO
ONLY A VISCOUNT WILL DO
ONLY A MARQUESS WILL DO
ONLY A LADY WILL DO

A Time Traveler's Highland Love Series
TO CONQUER A SCOT
TO SAVE A SAVAGE SCOT
TO WIN A HIGHLAND SCOT

Time Travel Romance
DEFIANT SURRENDER
A STOLEN SEASON

Scandalous London Series
A GENTLEMAN'S PROMISE
A CAPTAIN'S ORDER
A MARRIAGE MADE IN MAYFAIR
SCANDALOUS LONDON - BOOKS 1-3 BUNDLE

High Seas & High Stakes Series
HIS LADY SMUGGLER
HER GENTLEMAN PIRATE

HIGH SEAS & HIGH STAKES - BOOKS 1-2 BUNDLE

Daughters Of The Gods Series
BANISHED-GUARDIAN-FALLEN
DAUGHTERS OF THE GODS - BOOKS 1-3 BUNDLE

Stand Alone Books
TO SIN WITH SCANDAL
OUTLAWS

ABOUT THE AUTHOR

Tamara is an Australian author who grew up in an old mining town in country South Australia, where her love of history was founded. So much so, she made her darling husband travel to the UK for their honeymoon, where she dragged him from one historical monument and castle to another.

A mother of three, her two little gentlemen in the making, a future lady (she hopes) and a part-time job keep her busy in the real world, but whenever she gets a moment's peace she loves to write romance novels in an array of genres, including regency, medieval and time travel.

www.tamaragill.com
tamaragillauthor@gmail.com

Made in the USA
Las Vegas, NV
18 March 2021